Lock Down Publications and Ca$h
Presents

DRILL CITY 2

DOUBLE CROSSED

Written By
ZAY'TOWVEN

First Edition 2025

Printed in the United States of America

Lock Down Publications
P.O. Box 944
Stockbridge, GA 30281
www.lockdownpublications.com

Like our page on Facebook: Lock Down Publications
www.facebook.com/lockdownpublications.ldp

Stay Connected with Us!

Text **LOCKDOWN** to 22828 to stay up-to-date with new releases, sneak peaks, contests and more…

Like our page on Facebook:
Lock Down Publications

Join Lock Down Publications/The New Era Reading Group

Visit our website:
www.lockdownpublications.com

Follow us on Instagram:
Lock Down Publications

Email Us: We want to hear from you!

Chapter 1

6 MONTHS LATER...

The table was full of cocaine, a Drako sat on the side of the couch. Willy Key was in the kitchen whipping up a couple ounces of crack; he was the best chef in Rockford—the spot was rented his name. While Willy Key might've smoked crack, he helped tremendously in getting all the customers to the spot. The door was constantly swinging, with Zaro having just dropped half a key on us a few days prior. I rose from my seat and grabbed the Amiri bag of money, containing 100 bandz, which was all the money we'd made for the week. Zaro usually sent Zoo once a week to do the pick-ups, but this time I was to drop it off myself, as we had to talk anyway . . .

"Aye, I'm 'bout to drop this bread off. When you down cooking that shit up, put it in the safe. I'll be back shortly," I said. Willy Key knew not to do anything stupid. Everybody in the streets knew Switch Gang Family wasn't to be played with. We'd gotten the name after the spat we'd had with a few niggas. Out here, when you send 50 rounds or better at your opps, you make a name for yourself. Everybody knew we had them switches on deck.

As I moved towards the door, out of nowhere its hinges flew open. While it crashed to the floor, a stampede of men trampled over its remains . . .

"DEA! POLICE! DEA! On the ground!" the men yelled as they entered the apartment.

They came in with full tactical gear, their AR-15s trained on anything in their path. I dropped the bag of money; my first thought was about all the dope that we had in the house. Willy Key was already on the move and could be heard in the bathroom flushing the drugs down the toilet. I stood, frozen, with my hands in the air, looking stupid. I shook my head because they'd caught me slipping . . . shit was all bad for me. As I laid on the ground, the police put me in handcuffs, then one of the officers got close in my face and spoke, "Where's your boss man Zaro?"—his breath smelling of salami meat.

"I don't fuck wit' swine pig," I shot back as the cop reached up to slide his mask off.

"You know who I am?" he asked.

I shook my head. "I don't give a fuck who you are."

He smiled. "You'll care soon enough, asshole," he said before walking off. I stared at his back, wondering why he had said all that. I purged the thought to focus on the present. I had other shit going on right now. One of the officers came out from the kitchen parading a bag with 20 fresh-cooked oz's of crack. The officer held it up like he'd found a winning lottery ticket at the end of a rainbow . . .

"Look what I got. He ain't flush everything," the man said whilst dangling the Ziploc bag in front of me.

I dropped my head, defeated.

"Looks like a life sentence to me," another cop jeered.

"Fuck you, take me to jail," I said.

Mr. Salami-breath looked at me with a hard stare before speaking. "You'll be begging to talk to me, just like your friend O'Riley did. Oh, and just when you finally think you got my undivided attention, I'm gonna make you give up your own mother for another friend. Trust me, you will," he said cockily.

Who the fuck does this guy think he is? I thought to myself before wondering how the fuck he even knew O'Riley; he'd been locked up going on six months now since we'd taken over Waaco.

“Get his ass outta here,” the cop said sharply.

I was led to a nearby squad car, and when we arrived at the precinct they sat me in the narc unit for some time. They had all the drugs, guns, and money. I knew Zaro would be furious because he'd asked me to get the money to him days ago. I hadn't gotten around to it because I was preoccupied with way too much other shit. Willy Key had just finished cooking 5 zips, and there were 2 Drakos and 2 Glock 19s in the house. I hadn't thought of the severity of what I was facing until I was uncuffed and had the cops escorting me through the hallway. As we finally arrived at the end of the road—a door reading *Interrogation Room #1.*

“Have a seat,” the man said.

I plopped into the chair as the cop sat across from me.

“I'm Detective Curly Abotts, and this is my partner Coats,” he said while his partner entered the room. I recognized them both from the house raid. It seemed Mr. Salami-breath was Abotts.

“I ain't got no rap for neither one of you mutha-fukas, so you can take me to lock-up. I ain't with all the bullshit,” I stated.

“That's fine. I know you're a nobody anyway. It's your boss I'm after—Zaro. That's his name, right?” he inquired.

I looked at him with a confused glare and wondered how he knew Zaro; this was getting really odd now.

“I need an attorney, sir,” I said politely.

“That you're gonna need . . . especially for all that dope we just got you with,” he said before standing up to leave. He walked out, leaving me there to think. I hoped Willy Key didn't snitch me out. He was older than me, so I'm hoping he stuck to the code. They'd separated us when we got downtown, but in the back of my mind I could see him somewhere snitching.

I was transported over to the jail, where I got booked in. Illinois had this new law which forced me to wait on a judge to grant me bail. My court was the next day, so I had to lay low until then. As I got to the holding cell, Willy Key was laid out on the bench, his hair matted to his head.

"Man, get yo ass up. How long you been here?" I asked, and before he could answer I continued, "I thought you were in the narc building." I was actually kind of shocked to see he was already there before me.

"Man, I told them cracker mufukas I ain't have shit to say, and they brought me straight here," he said, speaking like a true soldier.

I still didn't know if I could trust him, even though he didn't cross me as the type to rat a nigga out. The thing about addiction is, it fucks with your loyalty. He been smoking crack like 90 going north, and from my experience, it's hard to trust a drug addict.

I picked up the phone to make a collect call to Zaro. Willy Key laid back down, looking comfortable; he was used to being in jail. This was a first for me. The phone rang out—I got no answer. That was some bullshit. I continued to blow his phone up but got no answer.

"Give it up for now, young blood. We gone be here for a minute. You might as well relax," he said in the middle of his little nap . . . I looked at him with a side stare.

"Not me, OG. Nigga betta come get me outta here, for sure," I said sternly.

"Or what—you gone bend the bars and go find him on your own, then try to kill him? You can't help what you can't control, so just sit back and let the situation play out."

I looked at his calm demeanor, but the thing is, we got jammed with so much shit—shit that Zaro had warned me about. The money shouldn't have been there for one, though I couldn't help but to ponder how I was slipping. While this was going through my head, I hoped no one else would see it.

"It is my first time in jail, OG. What they gone do to us?" I said.

"I know it may be over with for me, but they gonna charge us both with the entire house. I'm guessing whoever was closest to what gets charged with it. So, since I was in the kitchen, the 5 zips of hard was mine, with the other half-key of powder being yours. The guns were closer to you, but what got me is they claimed to have found some meth. I ain't never seen none of that shit before."

"Was it a lot?" I asked curiously.

"No, it was just a user amount. I think it was two 8-balls."

I dropped my head, thinking about how this all could that have happened. I didn't tell Willy where it had come from though.

"How much time does that carry?" I asked with caution.

"Fed time."

The C/O came to take us to our pod. They had us take a lice shower then led us to the pod. It was late night by the time we'd gotten there. The cops were cool and they let us be cellies. I walked into my new home and set my things down; the cell was disgusting, but Willy let me have the bottom bunk.

The next morning came quick, we both had to see the judge in order to get a bond. They gave us breakfast before the C/O came to take us off to court. After we came back it was time for dinner and I didn't even bother to get my tray, I went straight to the pay phone to try Zaro's number, but this time it gave the message that it was off. "Dam," I muttered then slammed the phone down.

Heads turned my way as I walked off heated. The judge hit me and Willy with a fifty rack bond to touch the streets. Willy strolled up, mouth full of food, like it was nothin'.

"Calm down, youngin', ya man gone reach for you."

Just as he'd said it, the C/O yelled out for Willy. We both turned our heads, shocked.

"How the fuck you getting out?" I asked, surprised, and slick mad that they hadn't called me.

He shrugged. "I ain't gone ask no questions."

I stood there stuck, mind twisted, tryna make sense of it all. Slid back to the cell, just moping while he packed his shit up. Right when I was 'bout to spazz, the C/O called my name—had me jumpin' up like a rabbit.

(ZARO)

KAMAR'S CAR LOT 6 MONTHS AGO...

Zoo and I walked in, not giving two fucks about killing nobody inside the shop. I was prepared to stand on business if this meeting didn't go my way. I walked in, looking at all the added security they had posted up *everywhere*, and touched my glizzy. As we walked to the end of the hallway, I was granted access to Kamar's office with no friction whatsoever.

When I walked in, he sat behind the desk blowing cigar circles in the air, with an Arabic man seated next to him. The look he had on his face had changed somewhat; it was still menacing, but this time it had a hint of relaxation. I still wasn't about to let my guard down though, and Zoo stood at my side ready to go.

"Was up, unc? You called me here to watch you smoke cigar circles?" I said, looking from him to Saleen nervously.

He leaned forward. . . "First off, you ain't have to bring ya dogs," he said, then pointed to the screen. The Muslims had their weapons trained on Telay Nem. They had the up's on us for sure.

"A'ight, so what you want, big dawg? You called me," I said, frustrated and ready to get whatever it was over with.

Saleen sat on the edge of his seat. . . "Flex is dead, and the Waaco drug market is open. He was a top earner," he said.

I looked down at his feet and noticed the duffle bag.

"I heard. What's that got to do with me?" I asked sharply.

"You just filled his shoes. Waaco is yours," Kamar replied.

Saleen picked up the duffle bag, then sat it on the desk. . . "This is 9 kilos. I'm expecting 50 thou per key. As it's more potent than what Shareef would pass to you, it will hit harder than usual," Saleen said.

I didn't know how to respond. 9 kilos was a lot of weight for me to move, and I wasn't used to that much dope at any one time. My plans in my head didn't reach this magnitude. I only wanted to take Flex out and live at the top of the throne. Right now, I was being fast-tracked into a life that I wasn't sure I could live up to. I stared down at the bag of dope, then looked at Saleen. . .

"With due respect, I don't know if I can take that. You're telling me that I owe almost a million dollars, and that kind of money takes time to come by—especially for me. I don't have clientele of that height, and Flex had Remo helping him, so they were spread out. I just got this little spot on the South, and it's doing good, but not good enough for me to put 9 kilos of D in," I explained.

Kamar chuckled. "You don't have to worry about that. The clientele Flex had will be yours too once you plant yourself inside of Waaco. The dope will sell itself, and the extra shit I'll help you with. There's a few people I want to put you in tune with that could help you get the product moving."

"You have ample amount of time to get the money up, as we're going through a down period at the moment. It's an understanding amongst everyone that it's a drought right now, which means you got 3 months to off the 9 kilos," Saleen said, reassuring me that I could handle the situation.

I paused to let the whole thing resonate with me. As the pieces fell together, I realized this was the life I'd been chasing, and with Flex out the way, it was an open lane for me. I looked at Zoo and could tell he was biding for me to accept, then I exchanged glares with Kamar, and he smiled at me. . .

"What's to think about, my baby? You got to eat," he said, then leaned back and blew a cloud of smoke in the air like the boss nigga he was.

I unzipped the bag. "You said I got 3 months?"

Saleen smiled, then rubbed his hands like a fly. "3 months. After that, you'll speak with my connection. He'll take over for Shareef. You'll never see me again unless you're called upon."

Kamar stood up quick. His look had changed swiftly. "Yes, but he doesn't have to worry about that, right?" he said, staring at Saleen for some sort of confirmation.

It sent me for a loop—I was curious what it all meant.

Saleen responded smoothly, "We'll cross that bridge if we get to it. . ."

I nodded and snatched the bag up.

"I'm throwing a party in a couple months, something I do every year. It brings the city out, and you'll be able to rub shoulders with some people—and I'll even set you up with the clientele. You don't have to rush, am I right, Saleen?" Kamar said.

"That is right, my friend. The 3 months is when the drought will be over, and your new connection will take over for Shareef," Saleen said.

"Okay, I'm good with that," I said, then Zoo and I exited Kamar's office with 9 bricks of raw dope.

BACK AT RENE'S HOUSE. . .

We all sat at the table. I had to come up with a plan to unload all this shit. Everyone looked to me for the answers, and with Flex out the game, our traffic was guaranteed to pick up. . .

"Telay, I'ma need you to hold down the East Side and make that nigga Willy Key put in some overtime getting that crack off. Remember, we got to come up with a M," I said, then looked to Bang. "And you gunna run Rene's house with me. This about to be the top spot in the town. We got to make sure it's secured, so Zoo—you keep security. It's gon' be some haters that want to see us down," I said, looking around at all the members.

"Damn, my nigga, we are about to be *all the way up* now. These niggas ain't gon' be able to touch us, gang," Telay replied.

"Oh shit! I almost forgot Cowboy out the coma," I said.

Bang smiled—he was ecstatic to see Cowboy back in the fray, as they were best of friends.

"Why we ain't at the hospital to see him?" Bang asked.

Rene walked in while we had our meeting.

"You got a new product?" she asked.

"Yeah. I need you to recruit more people to work the lab for us. We're about to expand to Waaco soon. You're a part of this family now. You ready to put the work in?" I replied.

Rene looked at me with a serious stare. It almost appeared like she was about to tear up.

"Honey, I ain't been part of nothing in a long time. This might be what I need to kick these drugs," she said with sincerity.

"That's good, because we about to start winning over here."

I scanned all their faces. The Switch Gang family was about to take over. . .

(THUNDER)

STATEVILLE PRISON PRESENT TIME...

I mugged the C/O as I walked out the final gate. He smiled at me. . .

"You'll be back," he said and chuckled.

I made a mental note to find his bitch-ass when I was settled in.

"Yeah, but watch *my* back for now, Officer Raymond Franklin—2234 Elm St., right off Pussy Drive!" I spat.

He looked at me, fearful that I'd known his real name and address. He and I were beefing on the inside, but I wasn't going to let it ruin what I had planned.

I walked to the Range Rover to see Calico. We slapped hands and embraced each other.

"It's good to see you out, my nigga," Calico said, genuinely happy to see me."It feels good to be out. But fuck all that, is the nigga who killed my cousin dead yet?" I said with venom.

Calico shook his head as we slid into the Range Rover. I looked him over—he looked like he was doing bad, not like all the pics Flex sent me at the joint.

He went into the stash box and handed me two Glock 10s. I popped the clips in and jacked one in the head. The rush of the metallic plastic in my grasp was definite, and I could feel the energy surge through my body; the streets was about to feel my wrath.

I looked Calico in the eyes as we pulled away from the prison.

"You got some explaining to do, my nigga. What's the deal with Waaco?"

"Some new niggas out there, they calling theyself SGF."

"Fuck dose that mean?" I asked.

"Switch Gang Family—but guess who runnin' the shit?"

"Nigga, stop wit' the story punch lines. Speak on it," I replied angrily.

"It's Zaro. Zamad's son. He top dawg right now."

"He's a fucking kid! You mean to tell me you let a child take over *our* projects?! You clown, my nigga. I can't believe you went out like a sucka. All the bodies we put down, and you get punked by some whiny-ass, bitch-ass adolescent—then let him kill my cousin!!" I spat, then punched him in his jaw while he drove. The punch caused him to swerve and almost hit an oncoming car.

Calico was like a brother to me, but right now he was acting like a sister.

"Fam, you—got to calm down and let me explain what exactly happened. You jumpin' to conclusions," he replied, holding his bloodied lip.

"Aight nigga, enlighten me."

"Flex and I robbed and killed the plug, but then they sent some Islamic hit team at us. They came on some real-life terrorist shit and murked like 15 of our people and—"

"Hold up. What about the nigga Remo?" I asked, interrupting his recant on the past 8 months.

"Remo was the reason we had to rob the plug. He ran off with 3 kilos and 100 banz."

"I told Flex dude was gon' be a problem. Where he at now?"

"I ain't been in the streets in a while. I got shot during the siege on Waaco."

I shook my head. All this shit was a big mess that I had to clean up.

"It's time we put the Wolf Pack back together and reclaim what's rightfully ours. Kato will be out in a couple weeks, so Waaco will soon be back under our thumb. And niggas gon' pay for killing Flex—*especially* Kamar. I know that slimey-ass nigga had somethin' to do with it."

"He's having a big party this weekend at the Colosseum. Everybody supposed to be there," Calico said.

"That's when I'ma pull up on that nigga Kamar—he'll feel more comfortable in his element. Take me to the Raq, I need a bitch," I said, then grabbed my crotch.

I hadn't had no pussy in years and was fresh home, so I was about to *punish* a bitch. . .

(COWBOY)

SAVON'S NEW HOUSE. . .

"Sis, we got to hurry up. I got to be at therapy soon and we already runnin' late," I said anxiously.

"I'm on my way, calm down," Savon replied, stepping out the restroom, hanging her earrings.

I sat in my wheelchair, waiting on her to wheel me out to the car. We'd upgraded our place in order to get a wheelchair ramp. I wasn't a paraplegic, but I was in recovery from several gunshot wounds.

Therapy was helping me get my strength back—not to mention I had one of the baddest bitches helping me recover.

Savon helped me into the car and we drove to the hospital. As we pulled into the front parking lot, I struggled a bit to get out the car when Crystal, my therapist, swooped in to help me out and wheel me through the lobby to the elevator.

The pool recovery center was on the 2nd floor, and it was equipped with everything I needed.

Savon worked at the hospital, so she went straight to work. She sent me a text asking about me getting home, so I hit her back on her line.

"A'ight, sis, Zaro said he'll come pick me up or my boo will take me home," I said playfully, looking up at Crystal with a smile stretched out on my face.

"Boy, you is funny," she replied and wheeled me into the pool area.

"I got to go, sis," I said and ended the call.

"You got me all to yourself," I said jokingly.

"You know how to make me smile. Let's get to work though—I need you to walk again."

Crystal was a huge help in getting me through a real tough time. We had a platonic relationship, but I wanted more. I'd changed a lot after being shot 3 times.

Crystal and I spent an hour in the pool, with her in that bathing suit of hers. I had to ask her out, but usually got discouraged by being in the chair.

If I asked tonight, I had it set in my head that I would shoot my shot.

As we exited the pool, I asked, "Will you give me a ride home?"

"You already know I will. You don't have to ask me that," she replied.

We both got dressed to leave, and by the time we left the hospital the sun had begun to set. She helped load me into her car and we rode off.

The car had an eerie silence, so I broke the ice.

"You should let me take you out sometime," I said, slightly shy.

"I'd like that. I've been waiting on you to make that move," she proclaimed.

It had been some months since I had to holler at a woman, and I was used to having both my legs functioning to do so. I felt helpless now, but I made sure not to let it show.

Crystal made me feel like a man instead of a cripple, and it made me fight even harder to get my legs back.

We pulled up to my house and she helped me inside.

"You want to chill for a minute?" I asked.

"Nawl, I can't stay. I got to clock out at the hospital—I'm still on the clock," she answered.

"Okay, so we gon' do something tomorrow?" I asked.

She looked at her watch. "How about tonight? It's still early and I only got 2 hours left on my shift."

"I'm good with that," I replied.

I was hyped on the inside. She agreed to show back up around 9 p.m., so I had a couple hours to get myself together.

There was only one problem—I had no money.

Zaro had hit me off with some of the robbery money, but I didn't want to accept too much. I didn't want to fall back into that lifestyle.

But I was down on my luck and broke again.

I hit Zaro's tag up and he answered on the first ring.

"I'm already on my way, gang," he said and ended the call.

Life felt funny—I was asking my friend for an allowance. This was something I had to endure in order to stay out of jail and alive, though.

I had too many brush-ins with the end, and God had spared my life twice, so I didn't want to screw it up.

I sat around and waited on him to show up. An hour passed when I heard a car door slam. I reached for my Glock 23 in the corner of my chair.

I still kept that fire on me because I knew there were people that still might want me dead. I wouldn't let it be that easy.

Zaro walked in, dressed down in an Amiri fit from top to bottom, sporting a big diamond Cuban link with the letters *S.G.F.*

Zoo walked in behind him with the same chain on. I admired their drip, but it wasn't something I wanted for myself right now. The drip felt off to me, as Zaro wasn't really the type.

We slapped hands. "What's good, gang?" he said.

I looked him up and down, then smiled. "Look at you, my nigga," I replied.

He grabbed his chain and smirked. "Nawl, this lil' shit ain't nothing," he bragged.

I remembered the times when something like that would move me, but now I was on the straight and narrow.

"Fam, I got a lil' situation," I said.

"Okay then, speak on it. Let me know if somebody fucking wit you—SGF gon' pull up," he said with a serious stare.

I admired Zaro for his newfound boss status—he held the title well. He wasn't the type of guy who let shit go to his head like other people.

I was always told how arrogant I was, and now with me being in the chair, I could see objectively. That's why I fought so hard for the change—it was all that I had.

"Nawl, ain't nobody fucking wit' me, but my pockets is gone. I know I said I didn't want none of that money, but I got this lil' baby that I want to take out. I don't want to keep asking sis for money—I know she prolly getting tired of it by now," I said.

"Gang, you was talking like it was some major. You helped build this empire too. I still got your cut whenever you want it. This shit is life, gang. Everybody eats. Ain't no man better than the next—we all equals, gang. This a dynasty," he said, then spun around.

"Grab that out the car," he said.

Zoo trotted off. He returned in minutes with an Amiri bag. I looked at him, then the bag.

"You *would* have the bag too," I joked.

He dug inside, then grabbed stacks of rubber-banded money and set them on the table.

"This should be 50 tho, that should hold you over for a while, right?"

I looked at it defiantly. "I didn't need that much," I said.

"It yours tho', fam, just take it. That should hold you over for a while."

I knew I needed that bread—it was the only thing gon' keep me from crashin' out. I snatched the stacks and stuffed 'em quick. Zaro ain't move, just sat there ice-grillin' his diamond-bustin' Rollie.

"You need to get you one of these," he said jokingly.

"Naw, thas yawl style, not mine."

Vrm—Vrm—Vrm. My phone buzzed. I checked the tag, it was Crystal.

"That's my date, let her in for me," I said.

Crystal stepped inside looking good as ever. I introduced her, "Crystal, you remember my brother Zaro, and this is Zoo, he family too."

"Oh yeah, Zaro you were at the hospital a lot when he was in the coma, how are you Zoo?" she greeted them politely.

"Good to see you again too Crystal, Imma need you to take care of my brother, he all I got," Zaro said.

"Don't worry, he with all state, trust me."

After the pleasantries we made our way to our cars. I looked at the Magnum Zaro drove, I didn't get how he was getting all this money and still drove an old car like that. I slid into the whip with Crystal, quiet but watching everything.

“So where are we headed?” she asked, settling behind the wheel.

“Let's go to the casino. I hear they got some good food inside and I want to see what it's like.”

The night looked promising, we talked all through our dinner and had a lot in common with each other. I was really falling for her. Her positive attitude about herself made me want to be around her all the time.

We touched down at my spot ’round 2 a.m.—night was well spent. When she helped me to the couch, my legs felt off, like they ain’t know what to do.

“What is it?” she asked.

“I don't know,” I groaned.

She rubbed my legs while looking me in the eye; I could feel an erection coming on.

“How does that feel?” she asked seductively.

I cracked a smile. "Feel like I got some strength in my legs . . . come help me up?" I asked, hype off the thought I might really be gettin’ my motion back. Me and Crystal been grindin’ for months, tryin’ to bring my strength back piece by piece. She eased me up slow—and I *stood* on my own, no help, no brace. Docs did say it might pop back outta nowhere.

I looked down . . . saw the boner pokin’ through my sweats, and couldn’t help but grin.

“It's a miracle,” I yelled.

Crystal giggled like a school girl. “Boy, you are funny.”

I hugged her, then walked across the room. After months of therapy, my legs were finally back and functioning. I eased back toward her, feeling like a toddler taking his first steps. She held her arms open, and I embraced the warmth of her body. She was soft as a baby's bottom.

We engaged in a passionate kiss; her tongue snaked its way into my mouth, the energy she radiated electrifying. We broke apart and looked deep into each other's eyes. I led her to my bedroom, my dick hard as a brick inside my pants. Months of lust-filled desires needed to be fulfilled.

I gripped her ass cheeks lustfully as we kissed. Crystal had a body type like Lisa Aries but looked like the Instagram model Shanina. She wasted no time pulling her shirt over her head. Her breasts sat perfectly in her *Calvin Klein* bra, and I admired the finely stacked DDs before me. When she released them from their captivity, I couldn't resist her almond-shaped nipples. She tilted her head back pleasurably while I nurtured myself like a baby being breastfed.

I licked around the circle, the brown shade at the center of her bosom. *"Uhmmmm! Oh yes!"* she gasped.

I laid her back on the bed as she assisted with wiggling herself out of her scrubs. She wore matching *Calvin Klein* panties beneath her pants, her pussy lips slightly exposed as I gaped at her vulva hungrily. She slid back in the bed, then curled her fingers for me to come to her. She moistened two fingers and began pleasuring herself until I couldn't resist the urge to taste her forbidden fruit.

I went down and gave her the thunder tongue, her juices flowing like Niagara Falls as I sipped her sweet nectar tastefully. Crystal grabbed my head and pushed her pussy into my face. It was an ecstasy that made me want to neglect coming up for air. I wanted to smell her until I was suffocated from her love.

After a few minutes of getting the best head she'd ever had, her legs trembled, and she tried to run backwards like Emily Rose in *The Exorcist*, her screams sounding like a loud banshee. *"Oooh my gawd!"* she cooed as she pulled me up face-to-face with her.

We engaged in a kiss, then I laid back on the bed for her to return the favor. She tugged at my *Nike* tracksuit, anxiously sliding it off me, then fished her little hand inside my underwear to find my pole. She gazed at the tip with tantalizing eyes, then dove in and sucked me whole.

"Uhm yes, you like that," she said seductively while licking the tip as if she were blissfully tasting an ice cream cone. My toes curled and scrunched in my socks. *"Yes baby! Damn, I've been waiting on this."*

The look she had in her eyes made my penis tingle, and I could feel my cum rise in my shaft. I tried to push back and get away from her suction; I couldn't afford to explode now, as I hadn't even got to the prize yet, and I yearned to feel her insides.

I flipped her over on all fours and mounted myself on her backside. I was in full control of my legs; it felt like I could run a marathon. Her backside was soaking wet. While she was sucking me off, she had been playing with her pussy. She took two fingers and spread her lips apart, giving me easy access as I guided my dick in with precision and skill.

Her moisture sucked me inside her hole just as a wormhole would do in space. She was slippery wet; her juice box squished and squirted as I plunged her in and out with a motion akin to the ocean. She arched her back up and reared like a raging bull.

"O yes! This dick is soooo good, daddy. Give it to me harder, daddy!" she begged and pleaded for more. *"Uhm! Give it to me,"* she moaned.

I could feel my pole jump inside of her, the tingle of cum back. I looked down to see her pussy oozing with cum. Crystal's pussy was wetter than any I'd ever had. She popped her head back, arched her back, and gyrated her ass in a circle. *"Ooh shit, this pussy good,"* I said, out of breath from pumping.

Suddenly, we both began to howl together. *"Oooo shittt daddy! I'm cuming, I'm cuming!"* she shouted.

"Me too baby! Arhhh shit! I'm 'bout to nut, damn!"

We sexed like two wild animals.

"I want you to nut on my titties," she said, then jumped up and got on her knees. She squeezed her breasts together and looked up at me while I stroked my pole. She held her mouth wide open, tongue out, eyes pleading.

I stroked until I blew my top and creamed all over her. She licked my cum from the tips of her tits. *"Uhm, tasty,"* she said seductively.

I lay in the bed out of breath and weak from the good sex.

(ZARO)

DOWN TOWN . . .

Me and Zoo was posted outside the county, burnin' time, waitin' on Telay and Willy Key to touch down. The bail people already told us it was gon' be a lil' wait, so we slid off, tapped in with Cowboy, and laced him with some paper.

But real talk—I wasn't even focused on all that. I had somethin' sittin' on my chest:

Telay.

That nigga been movin' off. Shifty. Like he tryna play ghost in plain sight. And I don't like that shit. He been fuckin' up in ways that don't even add up—sloppy ass decisions that ain't line up wit' how he used to carry it. I kept thinkin' maybe it was behind Tif gettin' clapped. But truth be told, they weren't in a relationship. Ain't no love story there. He mighta had a lil' crush on her dusty ass, but Tif was for the streets. Everybody knew that.

Still, death hit niggas different.

And ever since we all caught bodies, it's like somethin' in him cracked. Like he ain't built for this life no more. Niggas think catchin' a body gon' make 'em solid—nah, it just show you who really ain't.

Some wear it like a chain, heavy but proud. Others? That shit choke they spirit slow.

Me? I sleep like the reaper owe *me* a favor. Least that's what I keep tellin' myself.

I sat on the edge of the dusty-ass bed in that busted room, walls peelin', ceiling stained like old dope smoke. I stared down at the money sittin' in my palm—fresh, crisp, clean. Shit ain't feel real.

Zaro had thrown me a lifeline.

After that lil' stint up in the county, I realized real quick—I was down with a *winning* team. These youngins? Man, they came through and bailed me out, dropped big bread on a washed-up crackhead like me. Ain't nobody else ever did nothin' like that for me.

Not my family.

Not my so-called friends.

Nobody.

This was more than street shit. This was a *movement.*

I kept starin' at them blue notes, feelin' the pull—*that pull.* That pipe was callin' my name, loud as fuck, like it had a damn megaphone in my ear. The crave gripped me hard, like a cowboy ridin' a wild-ass bull, and I was strugglin' not to get bucked off. My demons was dancin' in my head, laughin', beggin' me to fall back into that dark.

But I couldn't.

I *wouldn't.*

I gotta change, man. Gotta flip the script for real.

My daughter don't see me as nothin' but a lowlife thief, straight-up junkie. She won't even let me see my grandbabies, and honestly? I don't blame her. I done stole, lied, disappeared for days behind a hit. I done did dirt. Hell, I *was* dirt. But I'm tryna come up out that grave.

This right here? This paper in my hand? This was my chance to rewrite my whole story. Not for the streets. Not for Zaro. But for me. And maybe—*just maybe*—my grandkids'll get to know a version of me that ain't got a stem in his mouth and guilt in his eyes.

I folded the money, put it in my pocket, and stepped out the room to walk to the *Walmart* across the street. Any other time I would've came in to steal somethin', but today I picked up a cheap phone and made my way to the food aisle.

I walked right past the whiskey aisle—even though I needed a drink—'cause I needed this to be a day of sobriety.

I paid the clerk for my food and went back to my room to set up my new phone and call my daughter.

"Hello," she answered in a calm, mellow tone.

I sat speechless, scared to speak.

"*Hellllo*," she repeated.

I cleared my throat. "Injah," I said timidly. We hadn't spoke in months.

"Who is this?" she asked.

I got scared and ended the call.

I'll just drop the money in her mailbox, I thought. I couldn't accept her harsh rejection.

I fixed somethin' to eat and went to bed for the night, wakin' the next mornin' feelin' refreshed and ready for anything.

Zaro pulled up on time, and as I came out, the windows on the car was dark tinted, so I couldn't tell who was drivin'.

As I got to the car and slid into the front seat, I saw it was Zoo drivin'.

"Was good, ole head," he said and slapped my hand.

"Not too much, ready to work. What y'all got for me today?"

"You know how to shake the dog up?" Zoo asked.

"I used to back in the day. Can't be that hard," I replied.

"A'ight, good. You gon' be in the lab with Rene for now."

He pulled into what used to be Waaco and parked in a buildin' by the back gates. We both popped out in unison, and I followed him into an apartment on the 3rd floor.

He knocked on the steel door. A woman answered and greeted him as we walked in.

The woman looked me up and down like she was tryna figure out what to do with me. Her and Zoo spoke outta my earshot, and I could tell she was thrown for a loop by my presence here.

Moments later, she stepped back inside and Zoo exited the apartment, leavin' me standin' with the woman who reminded me of the *Wicked Witch of the West*.

"So you're Willy Key. You ever shake heroin before?" she asked.

I nodded.

"What's the matter, baby—cat got your tongue?"

"Nawl, what more you want me to say?" I replied.

"Well, you ain't gotta be all rude, Willy. Come on here," she said in her aunty voice.

I followed my new supervisor deeper into the apartment. The place looked like a damn drug assembly line.

I couldn't believe what I was seein'. There was a mountain of powder along the table with four other women assistin' the makeshift line.

"Imma put you on cappin' the dope," she said, pointin' in the direction of a bundle of pill capsules.

Rene sat me down and showed me how to cap the first five packages, then left me alone to bid the rest.

I sat and bottled dope for hours while Rene walked around the room, makin' sure everybody was in line.

Nobody talked. We just worked.

Rene had told me my shift would be over at 3 a.m.—we was workin' sixteen-hour shifts.

Everybody wore masks in the house except for Rene. She loved the smell.

There was so much dope in that place, a nigga could easily catch a table habit just breathin' the shit in.

As I sat and bottled what was in front of me, I thought of my daughter—and how I would show up at her doorstep bearin' gifts.

Somethin' I should've done a long time ago.

(O'RILEY)

WINNEBAGO COUNTY JAIL FED LOCK UP . . .

As the C/O walked in with lunch, everyone rushed the door like hungry pitbulls.

I was starting to give up on Curly—he hadn't seen me since I been in this hellhole, and it was going on 3 months. Hopefully I'd remain safe.

Turns out Ralph's stint in jail got extended too, ‘cause he assaulted a cop.

I picked up my tray and looked down at it. They never served anything good. I couldn't choke it down; the food came from a company called Global that served the best mystery meat a garbage can'd ever tasted. I'd already lost 20 pounds during these 3 months, but still gave my tray to Ralph per usual before going to my cell to sit on the bed and stare at the wall.

I heard the C/O come back to the gates, and this time my name was called. I got up hurriedly to see what they wanted, despite knowing it couldn't be for bond, as I didn't have one. They'd got me on that prick Roger’s murder and some RICO shit. All the charges stemmed from Marty, and the way it was lookin’, I would die in here.

I also had a public pretender, ‘cause no real lawyer in town would touch an informant like myself, so I had to figure it out on my own.

Charles Wiggins met me at the gate.

“You got an attorney visit,” he said while unlocking the gate. “Go put your jumpsuit on.”

Wiggins was a dickhead towards me. I didn’t know why me and the guy were enemies—we just were.

I did as he asked and returned moments later to have him escort me out into the hallway and pat search me.

“Put your hands behind your back,” he said sharply, like he was some sort of drill sergeant or somethin’.

"You ain't got to be so tuff all the time, Wiggins," I said as we walked down the hall.

"Is that a threat or do you want a few nights in the box? Let me know what you wanna do," he barked.

I looked away and kept my mouth shut as we walked past the layers of rooms. I knew what that meant . . . it wasn't a real attorney visit. This was a cover-up for the police; I was being led into what people called *The Mouse Trap*.

I stepped into the room to see Curly Abotts sitting on the other side of a small table and foldout chair. Coats stood next to him lookin' like the RoboCop he was, and there was a folder sitting on the table.

Coats smirked as I entered the room.

"Have a seat," he said.

I took my seat, hating the look on his smug face right now. I needed him though, as I wasn't prepared to live my entire life behind bars.

Coats leaned in and spoke. "You don't look happy to see us," he said with his nerdy-ass voice.

"Cut the bullshit. I got what you want. Can you please get me outta here?" I replied, combatting their bullshit antics. I felt as though I was being patronized.

"Let's get to business. First, what do you know of this Zaro kid? His name has come up in a lot of our investigations—mainly shootings from guns that *you* sold him," he said.

I looked at him strangely, wonderin' how he'd even obtained that info. It finally dawned on me that Marty had come to him with his own version of the truth.

I chuckled. "Yes, I sold him the guns. Then he tried to pay me with money from a bank robbery, of which I believe he did."

Coats and Abotts both got closer at the mention of the bank. I smiled on the inside, knowin' I had their attention.

"Are you speaking on the Lawndale bank job?" Abotts asked.

"It's the only one," Coats interjected.

I went in and told them everything I knew about it, which wasn't a lot. Coats pulled his phone from his jacket pocket and showed me video of the robbery.

"That's him, and those are the guns I sold him," I said.

"What about this one?" he said and showed me another video, which looked like footage from a door cam. It was graphic and gory, with a young woman gettin' her brains blown out in front of her car.

"That's one of the Glocks I sold him."

Coats' eyes got beady. "Who is the shooter?" he asked.

"That's Zaro. The same person in the bank robbery."

They both sat back in their chairs.

"Now that we got the easy shit out the way, tell us about your Irish mob buddies," Abotts asked, like a sexual predator baiting a twelve-year-old schoolgirl.

"I gave you a taste of what I got, now you gotta tell me what's in it for me. I wanna get out of here *today*!" I said, and sat back like I held the power.

Coats looked to Abotts, and they had some sort of powwow with their thoughts until Abotts spoke.

"It'll take a few days. We gotta put some of these guys in the can first, but I promise you'll get outta here."

I huffed, then gift-wrapped the whole Irish mob, including the bikers. I spent 2 hours in the Rat Room and went back to my cell.

Ralph sat on the bed reading a book by Zaytoven.

"What did your lawyer say?" he asked, looking at me over his book.

Ralph was pretty much a square. I had a lot of long nights talkin' with him. Sometimes when a man got too much on his plate, he gotta share with others, so I'd told Ralph a lot of things too. I'd never tell him I was a rat, but he and I had become buddies. He worked at a lumber yard that was outta sight to my world, so I felt I could confide in him. He talked about getting home to his wife and kids—I felt empathy for him.

"Can I tell you somethin' without you runnin' your mouth to any of these clowns in here?" I said seriously.

"Come on, man, who do you take me as? We been cellies for a few months, plus you're the only one that's helped me since I been in this shithole."

"Okay, do you wanna see your kids a lot sooner?" I asked, thinkin' of a better way I could use Coats and Abotts to my advantage. If I could convince Ralph to help me build a story on the bikers, I could get him and myself out sooner, as they always need two to corroborate a story.

"Of course I'd like to get out of here. But how can I do that when servin' out jail time—and possibly more in prison?" he asked.

I stood up and looked at him to get a good read on his facial expressions, as I needed to know how he'd digest what I was gonna tell him. I scoffed, then gave him the complete rundown of what I had goin' on.

He looked dumbfounded as I told him about myself being an informant, but the second I asked him to join, he said:

"Where do I sign up?"

The glare he had on his face said he was in ten toes down, so I could play this to my advantage.

"There's this biker named Bruiser, with a partner by the name of Steve. You ever heard of the Devils Angels?" I asked.

He slowly and hesitantly shook his head *no*, so I went into depth about the situation and what I needed him to tell Abotts and Coats.

(ZARO)

2 DAYS LATER . . .

I carried the duffle bag down to my basement and went into the safe; it was full of all the money I had been busy stacking from the heroin. I looked inside the safe and noted I was down to the last kilo of dog. Saleen hadn't called for the re-up or even his owed money yet, and I was starting to get antsy.

I put what I owed him—the hunnid thousand—in the safe and exchanged it for the last kilo of heroin. I took a deep exhale as I stared at the stacks of money, then slowly closed the door. I put the brick into my bag and walked upstairs.

My aunt met me in the kitchen.

"Hey, baby, come have some lunch with me," she said while shuffling around the kitchen.

I'd been in the streets so deep that I hadn't considered her.

"I'm kind of in a rush, aunty."

"Come on, you. Sit for a minute. I got some things I need to talk to you about," she replied.

Aw shit . . . here we go, I thought. As her eyes shifted to the bag, I knew I had to have lunch with her now.

I huffed, but she had me cornered, so I agreed—first taking the bag to my car.

We sat and ate fried tilapia and French fries. It was silent for a moment until she spoke.

"I'm moving back to California."

I had a mouthful of food when she said it, so I swallowed hard and replied, "When?"

I always knew this day was coming. She was never supposed to stay here long; it was only supposed to be temporary.

"I put my two-week notice in with my job, so that will be the time frame. The house is yours. I'm sure you can handle yourself now. I've done all I could for you," she said.

I nodded, and she touched my hand.

Vrm, vrm, vrm.

My phone buzzed, interrupting the moment. The caller was Zoo. I'd sent him to voicemail, so I already knew what he wanted.

"I got to go, aunty. I got some business to handle," I said, then started to leave.

"Zaro," she called out.

I spun around. "Wassup, aunty?"

"I know what you're out there doing, and I want you to be safe, please."

I nodded, then walked to my car and slid into the front seat. Moneybagg Yo's *"Me vs Me"* came through the speakers as I backed out the drive.

Before I even made it past the sidewalk, I was swarmed by blue lights. I checked my rear-view and saw a slew of police with their guns drawn in my direction.

I dropped my head in shame. "Damn," I muttered.

One of the masked officers was at my window with an AR-15 to my head.

"Don't move, asshole," he spat venomously.

"FUCK!" I shouted.

They went through the motions of me getting out of the car. I followed their commands, shaking my head. I glanced up at the house, seeing the front door off its hinges, and thought of my aunt's safety—and all the money that was inside.

Hopefully, they wouldn't find the secret room in the basement. When they came for my pops, they'd never found it.

I was put on a grass patch near the street curb as two masked officers stood over me, clutching their weapons.

I looked up at one of them.

"What's the problem here, sir? I ain't did nothing, and this ain't no drug house. You sure y'all got the right house?"

The masked man chuckled, then spoke.

"Oh, we got the right house. Pipe down. You'll get your chance to talk."

I looked off to the side, pissed that he'd checked me like he did.

As they led Sheila out, I noticed she wasn't in cuffs. I wasn't given a chance to talk to her, though, as I was picked up from the grass, my jeans dirty all over. He laughed, knowing how expensive my jeans were.

I was put in the back of a squad car and taken to the narcotics unit, where I was cuffed to a bench in what looked like a break room or somethin'.

I figured they must've been searching the house while I sat alone for Abotts.

Thirty minutes later, Telay was led in. I looked up at him; he looked like hell. Something was definitely goin' on with him—even his clothes were dingy, like he'd been up for days hustling.

They cuffed him to a bench across the room, and when the cop walked off, we started to talk.

"What the fuck happened?" I asked.

"Nigga, they raided granny house."

Before I could respond, the officer led Bang inside. He was cuffed on the other side of the room. They were rounding my whole team up. I couldn't figure out what all this shit meant, or how they'd got on to us.

"Zoo been tryin' to call you and warn you about the raids. We were together when I got pulled over. I was caught with some bread and a little weed, but that was it. What happen wit y'all?" Bang asked.

"FEDs did a sweep—what it look like?" Telay stated sarcastically.

"But for what? Ain't nobody got caught up in shit, if that be the case. Cowboy, Nylon, and Zoo for sure would've been here by now. Didn't you say he was in the car with you, Bang?" I said.

Bang nodded. "Yeah. They let him go, tho'."

I sat back and analyzed which angle the police were tryin' to work on us. We continued talkin', tryna figure out what was goin' on, but were stumped.

Telay had been the only one in any type of trouble lately, and if he ratted us out for anything, they would *at least* have gotten all of us.

I pondered this until the pieces started to fall into place—but when I finally came to a realization, one of the dicks walked in.

He came over, uncuffed me, and led me down a hallway with labeled doors that said *Interview Room.*

We stopped at number three, and I was led inside and sat down in a foldout chair. Two men were already seated across the table as I entered.

“The man of the hour,” dickhead number one said.

“I ain't got shit to say. Call my lawyer.”

“You sure ’bout that? My name is Curly Abotts, and this is Martin Coats. My friends and associates call me Curly. How about you and I become friends? I can offer you a lot; I have some good men on my payroll.”

I laughed out loud, lookin’ straight in his face. I could tell he didn’t like that, as his face scrunged up and turned beet red.

“You’re gonna regret you said that. I got you on that kilo of heroin found in your car, which could get you a life sentence if it has traces of fentanyl. Oh, and here’s the second prize—we got your little crew on the Lawndale bank robbery too. I think your friend Telay would have somethin’ to say on that note, as he’s the one that got the other pending drug charges.”

Abotts leaned forward and pushed a manila folder in my direction. He opened it up and took out a photo.

“Or how ’bout this? If all else fails, you’re gonna wear *this*,” he said arrogantly.

I stared down at a gory photo of what looked to be Tif’s lifeless body and pushed it back toward him.

“Get me back to the holding area,” I said.

The policemen led me back down the narrow hallway. As I passed Bang in the hall, I nodded to him with a smirk.

They put me back in the holding cell with Telay. I looked at him, seein' if I could picture him ratting us out—but didn't get that vibe.

Bang was back in record time, so they grabbed Telay next. When the cop exited the room, Bang spoke.

"I ain't say shit. They was talkin' 'bout life and all that," he remarked.

"They tried me too, but I kept shit together."

"What about Telay?" Bang shot back.

"I trust him."

Telay was back in the room with us a short while later. I was glad to see no one else had been arrested, which meant Cowboy, Zoo, and Nylon would have to hold shit down for the time being.

Problem with Cowboy was, he ain't in the streets anymore, so it was really all on Zoo and Nylon. I needed them to handle shit, and wasn't sure if they had found the re-up money in my secret room.

After gettin' no information from all of us, we were transported to the county jail twenty minutes away. Once there, we sat in a god-awful cell that reeked of old corn chips and stale liquor.

We all got comfortable as I scanned the area for a phone. A lot needed to be done, and I knew Kamar could help us out. The phone was in the corner next to a hobo takin' a shit, so there was no way I was goin' anywhere near it. I shook my head.

"What we gon' do?" Bang asked.

"I'm going to call Kamar whenever dude gets done takin' a crap," I said, loud enough for him to put a rush on it.

"Sorry guys, I'm having withdrawals," he said back.

Once the guy finished, I called Kamar and he didn't answer. I figured maybe he didn't recognize the number or maybe it came up as a spam call, so I called Savon, and she answered first ring.

"Oh my God, I heard what happened," she snapped.

"Bullshit, I know. But listen—I need you to make this call a 3-way for me," I stated.

She agreed, and I gave her the number. Everyone sat on the edge of their seat as I waited for him to answer . . . none came.

She ended the call and tried it a second time—still nothin'.

"Where is Cowboy?" I asked, forgetting she was at work.

We ended up talking for the full 15-minute call period, then I called Nylon. He answered, and I gave him a list of things to get done.

I had to figure out how they got me on someone's door cam and who the informant was. All my guys were solid, so I didn't understand who it could've been. Whomever it was, they didn't put Cowboy, Nylon, or Zoo in the middle of it.

We had a rat somewhere, and it needed to be found.

HOURS LATER...

"Alright, ladies, let's find you a new cell to live in," the C/O said from the gate, waking everyone up. It had been a long, eventful day of not accomplishing anything.

The C/O dressed everyone in jail-issued jumpsuits, where we received a bedroll and were told to head to the housing pods.

"Form a single file line against the wall, gentlemen," the C/O ordered, actin' like a complete dickhead.

I took a chance and asked him to keep my guys together—it was about seven people in our group.

"C/O, can you keep us together, please? Us three here," I asked.

"My name is Officer Wiggins, and you go where this card says you go. Understand?"

This cracker was a straight-up racist, and I thought to myself, *If I weren't in this shithole, I prolly would've murked his ass.* I bit my bottom lip—it took everything in me not to spazz out on the clown.

We stopped at a pod, and he called all three of us by name. He'd sent us all to a unit together anyway. That was good.

With us being into it with them Waaco niggas, some of them might be in jail with us, and ain't no tellin' what might happen. Winnebago County Jail be goin' up a lot.

When we got through the gates, Wiggins hurriedly locked it back up.

Scaredy ass, I thought to myself as we entered.

I was approached by a dark-skinned guy with a low haircut and deep 360 waves. His jumpsuit was tied around his waist, exposin' his shirtless torso with a huge six-point star and the letters *THF*. That brand on his stomach, I knew, was a branch of Black Disciples—the group Lil Durk be rappin' about.

"What up, my name Dog. What y'all is?" he asked.

In the city, that meant what gang you was part of—and technically, we weren't part of any gang.

"SGF," I answered with confidence, readin' the confused look on his face. He was tryin' to make some sort of sense outta the information I'd given him.

"It stands for *Switch Gang Family,"* I added.

"What's that about . . . you know what, don't worry 'bout it. Only two cells open, so one of y'all can cell with me, and the other two take the cell on the other end."

Everyone in the pod looked at Dog talkin' to us—all them sizing us up.

I scanned their faces after dropping my belongings in my cell, then it was time to lock down for the night.

I lay in bed and stared at the ceiling, wonderin' how the fuck did this happen—then Dog spoke to me.

"What they get you for?" he asked.

"Shhh, a whole lotta shit, fam. Some dope, robbery, and a body."

"They got all y'all on the same shit?" he asked curiously.

"They got my nigga Neem on the robbery. I got the body and drugs."

"Damn, that's cold, my nigga. Good luck with that. You got a lawyer yet?"

"I gotta get a hold of my uncle tomorrow," I replied.

"What's your uncle name?"

This nigga was askin' me a lot of questions. I couldn't figure out why.

"His name Kamar," I answered dryly.

He stood up immediately, and I thought shit was about to pop off. Turns out Kamar was really a legend in the hood, and after I said that, I knew my stay in the county would be an easy one.

***

The next morning came fast. Court was early, and we went to get a bond—which didn't happen. Cowboy and Savon were there.

We got back to the pod disappointed. On top of that, the place got raided by a swarm of C/Os. Officer Wiggins picked *me*, of all people, to drag out into the hallway.

"You were the tough guy I brought in last night," he said.

I gazed around at the other officers and figured he was tryin' to make a scene.

"Wiggins, you need some help?" one of his partners said.

"Naw, I got this one. Come with me," he said, shovin' me in the direction of the laundry room, where there was another inmate washin' clothes.

He looked at me with a nod and smirk. "Grab the top mattress."

I looked at him confused, noticin' the mats were torn and dingy lookin'. I didn't wanna take that shit.

The laundry guy stared at me. "You might wanna grab it. They known for fuckin' shit up," he said.

"Let's move it—I don't got all day here," Wiggins said.

I was really startin' to hate that dickhead.

When I got back to the pod, the cops had fucked our shit *all* the way up.

I slapped the mat on the bed with a thud so loud I checked it for rocks or somethin'. I was shocked at what I dug out and looked around the room.

Luckily, it was just me.

In my hand I held a small touchscreen iPhone and 2 oz's of some kush with three large knives.

Vrm, vrm, vrm. The phone buzzed in my hand, and I answered it hesitantly.

"Hello?"

"'Bout time. You were s'posed to have this shit last night," Kamar said.

I smiled, knowin' everything would be alright now.

"Unc, I been tryin' to call you."

"Rule number one—no talkin' on the jail phones. Them cricket-ass cops tryin' to build a case on you. But don't trip. My lawyer, Frank Vela, comin' down today. We already talked, so be ready. In the meantime, don't give Wiggins no shit—he one of my people."

"You serious?"

"Chris Wiggins is his brother. You remember Chris, don't you?"

"Of course I remember. Chris work at the car lot, right?" I said with a broad smile—it was the first enlightenment since this darkness.

Kamar finished informin' me on what I needed to know, then ended the call.

I went and found my family in the day room, helpin' niggas clean up, while Dog played a game of chess.

(THUNDER)

CHIRAQ . . .

Calico and I drove around the city blocks in the Raq, the smell of fresh gun smoke fillin' my nostrils. I gaped at all the young niggas standin' out on the block.

Calico parked on King Drive, as we had a few hitters over there. I had to assemble the wolfpack; niggas thought they could kill my nigga Flex and walk the streets.

Rockford and Chicago had a long-standing beef with each other over who could kill the most, but over my nigga Flex, I was about to win this shit by myself.

After doin' a bid in Stateville Prison, a lot had changed. A lot of my niggas were either dead or in jail on a homi.

Everybody eyed the Range Rover as we parked. I hopped out and tucked my twin Glocks before approachin' the building.

All of a sudden, outta nowhere, we had *at least* ten sticks in our face, and I froze in my tracks.

"Fuck, you lost or some old nigga?" the dreadhead kid said, lookin' like he would squeeze the trigger with no hesitation.

I looked over to Calico with his hands up, positioned to get robbed.

I chuckled, then pushed the gun out my face.

"Nigga, go get Killa. Tell him Thunder out here," I said cockily.

The boy looked at me for some sorta recognition.

"You're Thunder?" he said, surprised.

I nodded. "Yes. Now go get Killa. We got shit to handle."

I was I' irritated at how disrespectful young niggas could be, but the men had lowered their weapons, knowin' they were in the presence of a BM.

Shorty that had the gun trained on me led Calico and me into the building.

It had been years since I'd been out here, and I looked around at all the new faces—they were all deceiving, conniving, and deadly . . . these were my type.

This was the wolfpack. All grimey niggas.

The hallways to the building were dark and dank. It reeked of urine, and dope fiends sat on the stairwells with needles in their arms.

I turned back to Calico. "Damn, I missed this, my nigga."

He laughed as we walked up the stairs.

"What's your name, shorty?" I asked as we climbed.

"They call me Pluto," he said as we got to the door.

He knocked, and a man with a MAC-90 stood in the doorway.

"Fuck you doin' up here, Pluto? You s'posed to be on perimeter," he said.

I stepped forward, and he clutched his gun as if to say, *Don't move another step.*

I inferred that shorty was I' handled by the nigga at the door, so I interjected.

"He brought me to see Killa. Now run along and get the boss nigga. Tell him Thunder at the door."

He looked me up and down.

"Oh shit, my nigga, I didn't even recognize you. When did you get out, fam?" the doorman said, leadin' us inside.

I recognized him as my nigga Chubbs. He was one of my top hitters, and I was told he was locked up on a double murder.

We embraced each other with brotherly love.

Killa yelled from the back after hearin' us talkin' and stepped out dressed in all types of designer clothes, diamonds 40ancing' around his neck.

I could tell Killa was eatin' good, while the rest of his crew's ribs were touchin'. I looked at him, disgusted at what I was seein', but this was someone I knew, so we clapped hands.

"What's good, my nigga? When did you get out?" he asked joyfully.

"'Bout a week," I said. And when we embraced with a half hug, I pulled my gleezy and put it to his thoughts.

"Nigga, your people starvin' in prison while you out here eatin'," I said venomously.

Calico drew his pipe in sync, just in case Chubbs didn't agree with my logic.

"You ain't gotta do this, big dawg," he said with a crackle in his voice.

Calico snickered at his cowardice.

"Boi, I *gotta* do this," I said as he shook his head.

Killa knew the trouble he was in. He was in the presence of death.

"I got 50 thou in the back I been holdin' for you."

I smirked. This nigga was a real sucker.

"Where is it? Let's get it," I said, annoyed at his fear. And to think this nigga name was *Killa*.

We had him in position as he led me to the back room slow. I knew he was plottin' somethin', 'cause Killa was a sneaky nigga, and I could hear the thoughts runnin' through his head.

We entered the back bedroom. I scanned the room as we entered, the bed littered with balled-up covers.

Killa went to the bed and was about to ease his hand beneath the covers when I snatched the covers from the mattress, revealin' five Glocks—all with sticks.

"Damn, my boi, you was about to do some dumb shit," I said.

He shook his head.

"Nawl, fam, the money in the box spring. I gotta move this shit out the way to get to it. They all on safety," he said, slidin' the mattress over to reveal a hidden compartment filled with stacks of money.

I curled my lip and chuckled when he spun around to face me.

"You can have all this shit back, my nigga—just let me go. Remember all we been through."

"I do," I said, then squeezed the trigger. *BOC! BOC!*

Just like that, I stood over his dead body twitchin' on the floor.

I hit him with two more shots. *BOC! BOC!*

"That's for lyin'. Glocks ain't got no fuckin' safety," I said, then left him in the bedroom—dead.

I got back to the living room and looked at Chubbs. He was so scared, the nigga could've pissed his pants. Calico kept his gun drawn on him.

"Put that shit up, my nigga. Chubbs ain't gon' do shit. Is you, fam?" I said, lookin' at him with a demonic gaze.

"Nawl, I ain't fuck wit' his scaredy ass anyways. We been tryin' to break free from that nigga," Chubbs said.

I could see the realness in his gaze.

"You wanna go to Rockford and put down some work in memory of the big homie Flex?" I said, lookin' at him seriously.

These lil niggas had to pay for what they took—and it was gonna be even worse if I found out they had anything to do with my nigga's death.

He nodded, and I knew he was gonna be down by law.

Killa's death would ring in the ears of all the cowardly niggas that used greed and money to control their soldiers. I hated that shit—and thought about murderin' that nigga my whole time in prison.

Pullin' that trigger sent a surge of energy through my body. It had been a long time since I had a kill with a gun. My body count never did stop while I was in the joint either—inside, niggas only respected violence too.

I had Chubbs gather up all the soldiers outside and let them know who the new boss was.

We met in the bedroom over Killa's dead carcass and looked down at him like he was a dead deer or somethin'. Everyone in the room knew that could've been them.

I gave my bit on defendin' Flex's death out in Rockford, and it seemed nobody wanted to work for Killa any longer. I had done the neighborhood a favor.

Now that I had my money right to fund the siege I was about to take, I had to come up with some guns.

I drew my attention to Chubbs, since he was Killa's top hitta.

"Where y'all keep the war chest? We got some bodies to stack."

Chubbs shook his head.

"Killa had us ditch them shits after we used 'em, so our supply ain't really up to par like that. Niggas got a few glizzies, but outside of that, everything we got is on us," he answered.

I'd thought Killa would've been a lot smarter than what he was. I guess greed'll get you every time.

I shook my head and thought for a minute, then ordered Chubbs to get rid of Killa's dead body.

I had to go find some guns—and I knew just where to start lookin'.

I made a call to Harley. He and I did time in Stateville together.

(THUNDER)

DEVIL'S ANGELS BIKER BAR . . .

Harley was a grimy-ass biker from the Eastside—a real cutthroat nigga who rode like the devil and lived even wilder. Him and his crew was like some modern pirates, takin' what they wanted and livin' with no brakes. Me and him got tight in the hole after shit popped off during a prison riot—his squad went at it with them racist-ass white boys, the Outlaws. I slid him a blade to finish one of them white boys off, and that shit sealed it—we was locked in for life. Now I'm here to collect on that favor he owe me.

The bar was set outside the city on a dirt road, secluded and off by itself. There were trailers and tents in the backside of the rather large bar.

Calico looked at me as we pulled up.

"Man, this look like some KKK shit," Calico remarked.

I laughed. "What, you scared or some?" I asked, lookin' at him with a smirk.

"Nawl, I'm just sayin' this shit look like some *Wrong Turn* shit."

We slid out the Range Rover and walked to the entrance. Bikes, new and old, littered the compound—some that looked like they been embedded in the land since 'Nam.

I clutched an *Amiri* bag that contained 50 grand. It was gon' be used to start our war chest.

While we walked in, they were playin' some old honky-tonk music, and the air was thick with cigar smoke, cigarettes, and a chemical aroma—most likely methamphetamine.

All the attention went to the two niggas that walked in, and Calico glanced in my direction. The music was turned off, and I could feel an uneasy vibe *emanating* from Calico.

Harley came from the back, pushin' his way through the crowd of people.

"Everybody get back to what you were doin'. These are my guests," he said in a raspy tone like he'd been smokin' cigarettes since he was two. He stuck his hand out for me.

"Was up wit' your peoples?" I asked, lookin' at all the menacing glares we was gettin'.

"Awl, don't worry about it. We don't get too much outside company, if you nawda mean. It's good to see you again."

"Likewise. Let's cut the small talk though. You got what I came for?"

"Depends on if you got what I want," he countered.

I patted the *Amiri* bag as my reply, and as he nodded, the chatter in the bar went back to normal.

"Come on, follow me," Harley said, walkin' with a light limp. He was a heavy, barrelly-built man with a long, dingy beard—kinda resembled a grimey, gritty-ass Santa Claus.

He led the way toward the back. They must've owned all the acres of land here, 'cause it was a huge complex. They had their own lil' city goin' on behind the bar.

There were a few trailers parked that looked like they came straight out a '70s movie.

We stepped into one of the RVs and saw an entire arsenal of weapons. I was amazed at what I was lookin' at.

I picked up a new *H&K* handgun.

"Is all these shits new like this?" I asked, admirin' all the Glocks.

"Most of 'em. What exactly you lookin' for?" he asked.

"I'm lookin' to take out a whole city block."

"As you may notice, you in the right place. I got enough shit here to go to war with Trump himself."

"You can say that again."

Harley and his crew could've started their own militia. I browsed the pipes like a kid in a toy store—it was too much to choose from. Even Calico lit up, his paranoia vanishin'.

"If you think this is some, I got some shit that's gon' make your willy stand up," he said, then went into a coughin' spasm like he had a hairball stuck in his throat.

We exited the trailer and he led us across the gravel. Dudes walked around us in lab suits—this shit was startin' to look dangerous.

"What they wearin' them suits for?" I asked, curious, as he led me to a large tent.

Inside was some crazy chem-set lookin' shit.

"I make my own blue dope," he said, as I tilted my head sideways.

"Meth," he replied, answerin' my thoughts.

He then led me to another tent.

"And this is what turns boys to men," he said with a smile, unveilin' a crate of hand grenades and RPGs. He even had C4—and that had me on edge and ready to go, 'cause this compound was highly explosive.

"A'ight, let's get to business. We definitely can use all this shit," I said, rubbin' my hands greedily.

(COWBOY)

DAYS LATER . . .

Nylon sat on the end of the sofa with a look on his face that screamed paranoia. He stood, then began to pace the floor and speak like a madman. I tried to calm him, but he just rambled on about not wantin' to go to jail.

The more he spoke, the more I convinced myself I should've never been a part of that whole robbery. I was good at gettin' myself in the middle of bullshit—and now I was in knee deep. Had I run inside the bank, I'd have been right along with them in Winnebago County Jail.

I don't know which charge is worse—kidnapping and holding hostages, or robbery. Maybe I was blessed for my role of not goin' inside, but I was still playin' tug of war. I thought changin' my life around would make things better, but it only soothed my conscience; my soul was stained, and there was no way I could go back to livin' the street life.

Makin' it out of the wheelchair was a blessin' from God, and with Crystal bendin' over backwards to help me, I couldn't go back.

We had begun to see each other exclusively and been stayin' with each other for some weeks. Her cousin Carl took care of her place.

Nylon plopped back down on the sofa and shook his head in defeat.

"We gotta do somethin' about this mess we in. Zaro said there's a snitch somewhere, so this shit could get worse if we don't find out who it is," he said.

"Damn! Damn! Damn!" I repeated.

"Yah, that's how I feel."

"If it's a rat somewhere, why ain't we in there with them?" I tried to reason.

It didn't make a lotta sense, so I sat and thought about the whole thing up to this point. Nylon'd been tryin' to get me to help him out with takin' over the business until Zaro got out, but I wasn't feelin' it—this wasn't my lane at the moment.

"You gotta help me, fam. I can't handle this shit by myself," Nylon said.

"What you mean? You got Zoo and Kamar."

"There's too much at play right now. You don't have a choice. If we can't find this snitch, we gonna be right along with them. Don't forget you shot Amy—or at least acted like you did—and that's attempt right there. You just as guilty as the rest of us, Reverend," he said sarcastically.

I scoffed and exhaled deep while bitin' my thumbnail nervously. He was right.

Nylon sat on the edge of his seat and in a low voice said, "Fam, we gotta find the rat and body whomever it is."

"It sound better said than done. It's gon' be like tryin' to find a needle in a haystack," I said, while suddenly havin' an epiphany.

Nylon took notice of the light goin' off in my head.

"What is it?"

"Amy. She's the only person that can possibly identify you and I."

"We gotta find her. You was s'posed to murk that bitch. Know this shit 'bout to come back to haunt us," Nylon stated.

This whole situation was gettin' deeper by the moment—and at this point, Amy had to be found. *This what I knew for sure.* The only way out of this was doin' the same shit that put me in the midst of it. I felt trapped, as I wasn't even sure Amy was the informant—it was just all centered on the robbery . . .

"We gotta find that bitch . . . and you gotta stop actin' pussy and help me find this bitch or you gon' be doin' a life sentence too. You and God could get real muthafuckin' acquainted with each other in the cell if you want," he spoke with agitation.

He stood up and grabbed his pipe, put one in the head, and walked toward the door while lookin' over his shoulder. He looked me square in the eye and said, "I'll be in the car," before hittin' the front door and leavin' me to make the decision of a lifetime.

Crystal and I had a bright future together. I was fallin' deep in love with her, and she was definitely wifey material—but how could I explain to her I had to jump back in the street?

It'd break her heart . . . but it'd hurt worse if she lost me to the judicial system.

I stood up and slid my hand inside the couch, grabbin' my Glock 23.

I slid into the front seat of Nylon's Hellcat.

"I knew you'd see this shit my way. Let's start with this bitch Amy," he said, then put the car into drive.

Big30's "Free Shiesty" blared through the speakers as we started toward Roger's house to find her.

There was no car in the driveway as we pulled up, and the house was dark. We drove past slow, both lookin' for any glimpse of activity. Amy was the only person that could link Nylon and me to the robbery.

The house looked to be vacant, like they'd moved. Newspapers even littered the porch, and the front lawn had grown wild—when before, it was well-manicured.

This house was our only lead, and seein' it made my bullet wounds itch. Findin' a middle-aged white woman was gon' be hard.

"What now?" Nylon asked as he continued to drive.

"I don't know. Let me think for a minute."

"A'ight. I got some shit to handle in the projects. You can slide with me," Nylon replied.

I looked at the time on my phone. "That's cool, but I gotta pick up Crystal from work. She wanna spend the night at her place tonight. She makin' me dinner."

Nylon looked at me and smacked his lips. "Ol' sucker-for-love-ass nigga."

(CALICO)

MEANWHILE BACK TO ROCKFORD . . .

I drove down I-90 with them shooters behind me, all of us hoggin' the highway in four black-on-black Trackhawks. I merged off on the first Rockford exit. Thunder rode with Chubbs in his Cadillac truck.

My time was up for now with Thunder—he'd had me on a mission since his release, and I had to get me some rest.

I drove toward Crystal's house. I hadn't been there in a couple weeks, 'cause she ain't been stayin' there much. She met some lil' young nigga that came through her trauma unit, and turns out she really liked ole boy—they was gettin' serious.

I know I should've at least gave her a heads up I was comin' by, but I was too tired to even talk to her. Plus, I still had a key.

Crystal had helped nurse me back to health after I jumped out the window in Waaco, and even hid me from them bow-tie killas.

I drove, listenin' to 42 Dugg's *"We Not Done."* The music had me geeked and wantin' to do somethin' before I crashed out for the night.

I made a quick stop at the *Stop-N-Go* down the block, walked inside, and purchased some snacks. When I got to the counter, I paid for some blunts too while flirtin' with the sales clerk.

As I walked to my car, I stopped in my tracks . . . I thought I'd seen a ghost.

I touched my waist, thinkin' if I had my gun on me.

Nigga betta be glad, I muttered, and continued walkin' to my car unnoticed.

I looked at Cowboy behind the tent. He was seated in the Hellcat and was so busy he hadn't even noticed me stalkin' him.

I thought about pullin' up on his ass and finishin' the job off, but I reached underneath the seat and chambered one in the head of my F&N. The stick on it stood extended far out the handle.

I looked around before the shots erupted.

Blocka! Blocka! Blocka! Blocka! Tish!

Bullets tinked the car as I slid my truck into gear.

Chapter 2

(NYLON)

STOP-N-GO . . .

While driving down 11th St., I spotted Calico inside a Quick Mart talkin' to a sales clerk. I couldn't believe my luck—he'd been outta sight since the bow-ties took out Waaco. He was busy layin' down some game to the sales clerk, so I had to take advantage of the situation.

I peered at Cowboy as I circled the block.

"You see that bitch-ass nigga Calico?" I asked, instigatin' him.

Cowboy perked up and scanned the area anxiously. "Where?"

"He was at that Quick Mart," I informed him, but by the time I got the words out, I was already pullin' back up to the store.

"What you wanna do?" I asked, grabbin' the F&N from beneath the seat.

Cowboy shook his head. "I don't think I'm ready for what I think you got planned," he said, a lil' tremble in his tone.

"That nigga tried to kill you, fam. You can't let that shit slide."

Cowboy huffed, knowin' I was prepared to ride him about not wantin' to take care of Calico. I wasn't scared—really just paranoid about all the cameras everywhere.

"If you won't, I will," I remarked, parking the car. I was gonna let Calico think we weren't payin' attention.

“I’m ’bout to use you for bait,” I stated, cockin’ the Glock 19 with the switch.

“What should I do?”

“Just sit there and look stupid,” I said, poppin’ out the front seat, Glock in hand.

I watched as Calico exited the store; he stopped and stared at Cowboy. I knew he was surprised to see Cowboy still alive, but he was about to be even more shocked when he got hit from behind with these rips.

Calico walked to the Range, still not noticin’ me stalkin’ him like a lioness predator. I hid behind a dumpster and waited for him to sit comfortably in his truck.

Bitch-ass nigga think it’s sweet, I muttered under my breath as I watched him lean forward in his seat. I figured he was grabbin’ his gun.

I crept up on him real slow and easy with my G19 out. I hit the switch to full auto.

Laddadadadadadadadadadadow!

The bullets whizzed through the air like balls of fire. The first few shots shattered the back window as Calico got low and floored the Range Rover, screechin’ tires as he booked it out the parkin’ lot.

Laddadadadddadaow!

I threw another 30 rips his way—my twin 19 spit venom on Calico’s Range Rover.

“Fuck!” I remarked, figurin’ I’d missed as he was exitin’ the parkin’ lot. I shot the glizzy till it was empty, then ran back to my cat and drove away.

“Did you get him?” Cowboy asked.

“Why you wanna know, choir boy? That should’ve been you blowin’ at that bitch-ass nigga, bruh.”

He sat there in his seat not lookin’ like the nigga I was used to. I needed Cowboy to shake outta this bullshit he was on, or we was gonna end up dead or in jail with the others.

He and I was all we had to put the work in and save the others.

I drove Cowboy toward his house to get his car so he could go pick Crystal up from work and enjoy his lil' dinner date.

We rode in silence all the way to his house.

"I'll hit you up tomorrow so we can finish searchin' for Amy. If you got any ideas, let me know," I said as we slapped hands.

I watched him slide out the front seat and walk to his Bronco before he pulled off.

I called Zoo to let him know I was on my way back to the projects.

(COWBOY)

MEANWHILE . . .

On my way to the hospital, I couldn't help but think of the shootout that just occurred. Now I had to worry about Calico huntin' me; I scratched my wound at the thought.

I tuned into Finesse2Tymes to help me get some good thoughts goin', but I had to get over this fear of usin' my weapon. Lyin' in that coma had instilled a high dose of fear in me.

I prayed for a change in my lifestyle, but deep down I knew I was driven by the anxiety of not knowin' where death was lurkin'. Bein' in a coma for a month gave me a lot to think about—and bein' too afraid and ashamed to admit that I was downright scared.

I arrived at the hospital and waited on Crystal to step out. Moments later she arrived wearin' her pink scrubs and Crocs. I admired her after-work sexiness as she walked up.

I smiled to myself, knowin' that I had a winner. She slid into the front seat lookin' like cotton candy.

"Hey, boo," she said and leaned over with a kiss.

I pulled out slow, not speakin' too much as we rode. She kept talkin', me givin' short replies. I feel she must've felt the vibe when she asked,

"What's up with you?"

"Nothin'. Just got a lot on my mind right now."

"Anything I can help with?" she asked, slidin' her hand between my legs, massagin' my inner thighs.

"Nawl, everything is good. I'll manage," I said, lookin' over at her with a lustrous gaze.

"Stop at the store," she asked.

The police had the mart taped off, so there was no way I was goin' there. She gawked at the store, wonderin' what happened. I didn't bother to tell her it was Nylon's work.

(CALICO)

That lil' bitch-ass nigga gon' pay for that fuck-up, I thought, heat boilin' in my chest as I hit Thunder's line. I put him on game 'bout what just went down, and he was *too* ready—talkin' 'bout *"let's slide now."*

I told him to chill, that shit could wait. I was drained, runnin' on fumes, and ain't have it in me to put no more work in tonight.

I whipped the wheel into the drive and tucked it in the garage. I walked 'round the whip . . . *Swiss cheese.* That bitch was riddled with holes.

"This outta commission for a minute," I muttered, rubbin' my jaw tight.

I stomped in the crib, sparked up a fat blunt, blew that bitch down to the filter, then collapsed on the bed.

I'll link with Thunder in the morning . . . and we gone bleed somethin' behind this.

(COWBOY)

I parked in her driveway, the house completely dark as we sat there. She looked at the door like she ain't even wanna go inside.

"What's wrong?" I asked.

She scoffed. "Uhm, nothing."

She stepped out the car as I started to discreetly grab my gun without scaring her.

When we walked in the house, I sniffed the air—it reeked of kush.

"Ugh, it stinks. Carl must be here," she said, then ducked off to the back room.

I heard her yell some obscenities, then she came back out to the living room.

"You okay?" I asked, a smirk stretched across my face.

"Yeah, let's go. My cuzin' back there high, so we can just go to your place," she said.

She quickly grabbed some food out the fridge, and we headed back to the car to drive to my spot for our dinner date.

(VERN)

DCFS...

We arrived at the Olson house in the early part of the day so we could be at the group home during school hours, so the other children wouldn't be present. Mrs. Olson gave us the grand tour of our new temporary home. I noticed the basketball rim out back — that was more my style. I would have someplace to shoot hoops.

Venture was the nerdy twin — he liked school more than sports — but Calvin, on the other hand, was a ticking time bomb. He was the reason we were getting kicked from every group home. Our social worker, Ms. Adams, had a goal of keeping us together, but she always told us eventually we would be separated. Both our parents were dead. There was no one that would take us in after those dangerous men had killed them. We were left to fend for ourselves. The system had labeled us as troubled youth.

Mrs. Olson led us upstairs to the attic, where there were six beds lined up — three on each side. I knew what that meant all too well. We didn't have any privacy.

"This is where you will sleep," she said as we sat our garbage bags of clothes down. We'd started with luggage carriers, but now all we had was the *system specialty* — black garbage bags.

Venture ran to the window.

"Mrs. Olson, where's the school?" Venture asked.

I glanced over to Calvin as he stood scanning the room like a robot.

"Please, call me Linda," she answered, while eyeing Calvin. "The schools are nice around here. You boys will fit in well."

I knew exactly what was running through her head, but also knew she wouldn't ask the question out loud.

"Can we have any bed?" I asked, anxiously wanting the one closer to the window to get a better view of the basketball court, seeing as that's where I would spend a lot of my time at.

She nodded and pointed. "Any three on that side — you can pick," she said, then spun around and exited the room.

We all took a seat on the beds when Ven looked at me.

"How long we gone be here?" he asked from across the room.

I shrugged and walked over to Calvin. I stood in front of him and fixed the collar on his Lacoste shirt. I had to look out for him, as Calvin had a quick temper, and I was the only one that could calm him.

As we sat in the room, a group of boys showed up. One boy looked to be about 13. He was heavyset and his whole stature said he was a bully before he even spoke. I spun to stare him down.

"That's my bed," he said to Ven.

My twin stopped unpacking and peered at him with a blundering gaze.

"But Mrs. Olson said we can have any bed on this side."

"That bitch don't run shit — I do," he said, using a mouthful of vulgar language. The boy cursed like a pro, and the way he dressed I figured he was some sort of gang member.

I walked over to him and got in his face.

"We don't want no problems. We were forced here too. Where do you suggest we sleep?" I asked.

"On the floor, pussy," he said venomously.

"Is Bobby bothering you boys?" Mrs. Olson asked, with her hands on her hips, frowning at Bobby.

He hung his head shamefully, then denied trying to be a bully. I didn't rat him out, I just kept quiet. Ven was about to speak up until I shot him a mean stare, so he kept silent.

Mrs. Olson scolded Bobby, then walked away feeling accomplished. But when she got out of earshot, Bobby got in my face.

"This my house. Y'all gon' do what I say," he spat.

I looked him up and down. He wore his hat cocked to the right and I could tell he thought he was some sort of banger. The other two boys with him must've been victims to his bullying because they didn't speak. It seemed he was here to recruit me and my brothers.

"Ain't nobody scared of you, Bobby," I said.

He chuckled, then strolled to his bed. While looking back over his shoulder, he pushed the mattress over and grabbed a small box-shaped gun.

I gaped at it fearfully, as I'd seen my dad with those things before. He always told me they were bad for me. Bobby tucked it in his pants.

"Y'all wanna join the G.D.'s? You can get money like me."

I stepped back and shook my head. I wasn't into gangs, and my father had always told me he didn't want that life for us.

I sat on the bed while Bobby circled me like a shark, until Mrs. Olson called for him. Then he went downstairs.

Ven walked up to me. "We can't stay here," he said with a serious stare.

"It's the only place we got," I replied.

"What about Aunt Karen?"

"If she wanted us, she would've taken us at the funeral. We all we got, Ven," I said, then walked over and hugged Calvin, tears welling up in his eyes.

"I wanna go home," he said, voice shaking.

I sat next to him with my arms wrapped around him as we hugged each other.

"We can't. Mom and Dad are gone, Calvin."

"No, they're not," he said, before going into one of his temper-tantrums. There was no way to control him when he got like this.

As I tried to calm him, Bobby walked back into the room and froze in his tracks, looking straight at Calvin. He eventually laughed — sending Calvin into an irate state.

Mrs. Olson ran into the room, first thinking it was Bobby who'd done something to him. But once we calmed Calvin down, we all got a chance to get ready for bed.

***

The next morning, everyone went to school but us; we hadn't been signed up yet, so we stayed home for the day. We sat around peacefully until 4 p.m. I sat on the edge of my bed and read Calvin a book while Ven sat by the window, looking over one of the schoolbooks.

Bobby stepped in with two boys at his side and walked over to Ven. He smacked the book out his hands and said, "That's my shit. I didn't say you could read it."

Ven didn't give in to his threats as he tried to move from his path, but Bobby kept blocking him off, punching at Ven's chest — until Calvin ran over and punched him.

"Leave him alone!" he said with a deep, threatening tone as he swung wildly.

Bobby tried to block, while the other two boys jumped in and we all got to fighting. Ven wasn't much of a fighter, as he lay on the ground crying while Calvin and I got pummeled. Bobby eventually whipped out his knife and threatened to kill me while he and his crew pinned me to the ground. The other two held Calvin's arms.

I kicked the knife from his grasp and it flew across the room as Calvin broke free. Bobby and I began to tussle again, when suddenly Calvin ran up and put the knife in Bobby's back. The sound of his bone cracking made me cringe. *Shhk! Shhk! Shhk!*

Blood spewed everywhere as Calvin repeatedly stabbed him while the other boys stood in horror. I grabbed Calvin and took the knife from him just as Mrs. Olson stepped in, mystified by what she'd seen — until she covered her mouth at the sight of Bobby's blood-soaked body.

She screamed for someone to call 911. Ven was balled up in the corner, scared, while Calvin stood like a madman — his chest heaved up and down with anger. The other two boys ran out the room to call 911.

I had to get Calvin out of here. I grabbed him by the arm and we ran from the house.

The neighborhood was unfamiliar, and the police would be looking for us too. We ducked into a garage and sat there for some time. Police had swarmed the house. We watched them from the dark and hot garage. I peeked out the window and watched the police scour the backyard.

"I'm hungry," Calvin said loudly as one of the officers passed the window.

"Shhh, you gotta be quiet," I said.

"I wanna go home," he said, not understanding the magnitude of trouble we were in.

We waited the police out. Then I snuck back into the house to get our things. Calvin lay sleeping in the garage as I went to the kitchen and raided the fridge. I got us some food to eat, then crept upstairs to what used to be our room.

Ven was lying in bed, staring at the wall. He peeped in my direction as the door creaked. I slid inside the room smoothly, and he sat up in bed.

"Vern, is that you?" he asked from the darkness.

I walked over to his bedside. "What happened?" I asked.

"They think you and Calvin killed Bobby together. Carl and Roni lied to the police — said it was you and Calvin's fault."

"What? Are you serious? What happened to them?"

"They went to juvie. Mrs. Olson had to go to the hospital 'cause she had a heart attack," he answered.

"Damn," I muttered, shaking my head.

I hugged Ven and told him he wouldn't see us for a while — we had to get someplace safe. We couldn't stay, or we'd end up in jail. So, after saying my goodbyes, I slid out the back door to the garage and left.

Calvin and I walked the streets for some time, with no destination in particular. As we walked down Forrest Hills Street, a police squad car drove past — then slowed down. I tried to walk normal until the car did a U-turn.

I pushed Calvin, but he wouldn't run with me. As the cherries lit up, the cop got closer, so we ducked into an alleyway. We hid as the cruiser drove slowly, shining its beams back and forth.

Calvin wouldn't be quiet, though, and he was about to get us caught up. I couldn't hide with him any longer. I didn't wanna go to jail — they'd have sympathy on him versus me.

Tears welled in my eyes as I hugged him.

"I love you, brother," I said, looking him in the eyes.

Calvin had no clue what was going on as the squad car got closer, but I knew I was on borrowed time. I sprinted from behind the dumpster, leaving Calvin. The cop car's motor revved to catch up — only to stop upon seeing Calvin sitting against the wall of a restaurant.

I ran toward the park in the dark, knowing I could lose them there. I hid under the bridge until I could clear my mind. I sat for a few hours, until I thought about a place my father had taken me a few times. He said it was the safest place in the city.

I arrived in Concort Commons at the break of dawn — though it was known to the streets as *Waaco*. I went to the back building and found a vacant apartment to sleep in peace.

(ZARO)

ONE WEEK LATER . . .

I walked to the front gate of the pod after hearing my name being yelled. C/O Wiggins stood waiting for me.

"You got an attorney visit," he said.

I looked at him sideways, like it was some sort of trick.

"Nawl, nothin' like that. It's a real one. Kamar sent you," he said.

I spun around to go put on my jumpsuit, then returned ready to go.

"I'm ready," I said, pulling my collar down as everyone yelled good luck—something the pod did whenever someone would go see a real lawyer, not go talk to some fake-ass cops.

I arrived at the interview room and saw a man sittin' with his legs crossed like an old pimp. He was dressed more like a model than an attorney.

"How's it going? My name is Frank Vela. Kamar retained me for your case and any future cases," he said with an overly perfect smile. He stuck his hand out for me to shake, and I was almost blinded by the Rolex he wore. I knew this guy didn't come cheap.

"Have a seat," he offered. I obliged.

"So I had time to look over your case," he said, unbuttoning his jacket, "and there's some loopholes I can use to get you boys outta here. However, there's something you may have to do to help me—if possible," he said, giving me a narrowing eye from over his *Ray-Ban* glasses.

"Like what?" I questioned curiously.

He opened a folder and slid it my way.

"I found out who the rat is. You know a guy by the name of Marty or O'Riley? They're Irish mob guys," he said with a stern gaze on his face.

The man suddenly looked like a dark figure, and I understood now why he was in front of me.

"Yeah, I know him. He helped us out, but he's not part of my crew, so he ain't got shit on us," I replied.

"Wellll, I beg to differ. This information doesn't come cheap either—but I'm good at what I do. O'Riley is here at the jail with you, so you're gonna have to figure something out about keepin' him quiet. *Kapiesh?"*

I nodded.

"One other thing before I go—I don't do proffers. I hate rats and I don't indulge in deals with law enforcement. You don't peg me for the type, but I wanna be clear. I'm representin' your crew as an entirety. I will only report to you, since you're the head of this ship. Am I correct?" He looked at me over the glasses again with the same narrowing eyes.

I nodded again.

"Good. If you can get to O'Riley, this little thing with the bank robbery will disappear. The murder of Tiffany Harris will be a little harder, but I'm sure it'll fade as well."

"A'ight, I'll do whatever it takes to get this mess cleaned up," I answered.

We finished our discussion and I signaled for the C/O, lettin' him know I was done with the visit. The C/O ushered me out the room and back to my pod, where Telay and Bang both stood eager, wantin' to know what happened.

I nodded for them to follow me to the cell to talk privately. We discussed everything I'd talked to Frank about, and everyone was taken aback by the fact O'Riley had snitched us out.

"What do we do now then?" Telay asked.

"We gotta try and get at that Irish piece of shit some way. He's here at the jail someplace."

Bang started to pace the floor.

Later that day, we were sittin' around playin' cards when the phone vibrated in my underwear. *Vrm, vrm, vrm.* I ducked off to the room and pulled it out. The tag read *Savon.*

I quickly answered. "Was up, baby girl? Everything okay?" I asked, peekin' out the door makin' sure I wasn't seen on the phone.

"I'm good. I was callin' to let you know that little phone you had me hold been ringin' since this morning."

I thought about it for a moment, then it came to me—it was the satellite phone that Saleen had given me when he gave me the dope to sell. This was good news, 'cause now I could re-up. Nylon, Zoo, and Willie Key were handling the spots for me, money was still rollin' in, but I had to run the operation from a distance.

I asked her to give me the number so I could call him myself.

She told me Cowboy was walkin' again—which I'd already known—but it was good to hear her again. We hadn't told him yet that her and I were a couple. I didn't know how he'd react to the situation, since he and I had been best friends for a long time. Even now that we were trappin' together, I didn't know if that was safe or not, so I opted not to tell him immediately.

She gave me the number, then assured me that she would be over to visit tonight.

After I ended the call with Savon, I called Saleen. He must've answered in Arabic because I didn't get the greetin' well—but what I did understand was he'd slammed me.

"Hey, this is Zaro," I replied.

"Awy, yes. How are you? This is not the phone I gave you," he remarked.

"Yeah, I know. I'm kind of in a sticky situation right now, I'm in—"

He cut me off. "I am aware of your position, my friend. I have eyes everywhere."

"I hope this doesn't have any effect on our business."

"Oh no. In fact, I was callin' to let you know my friend Ackmed has a package for you. Can you get the money down to Shareef's old spot? It's being ran by Ackmed now—he'll get you right. I'll text you his contact now," he said.

Seconds later, *ding*. Text came through.

Saleen and I talked more about our plans when I heard someone yell *"baked ziti!"*—which was the call that meant the C/Os had come to our pod.

I ended the call abruptly, not wantin' to get caught on the cell phone, then tucked the phone back in my underwear and stepped out into the day room.

Telay walked up askin' if everything was good, and I nodded before walkin' up to the cop and askin' him to get Wiggins down to the unit.

20 minutes later, Wiggins pulled me into the hallway.

"Was up, Zaro?" he asked.

"I need to find someone in the jail."

He looked around, knowin' we was 'bout to get into some shit that could put his job on the line.

"Who?" he asked, with shifty eyes.

"O'Riley—the Irish mob guy."

He let the name roll around in his head for a moment before he replied, “I believe he is on the other side of the jail.”

“Can you get him moved?” I asked.

He shook his head. “That may be hard for me to accomplish, but I’m sure we can figure somethin’ out.”

“Okay. We gotta get to figurin’. He’s my ticket outta this hellhole.”

“Give me a few days,” he exclaimed.

He opened the gate back, and I went back to the day room to let the boys know I had the situation under control.

Days later, we were watchin’ the news when it showed a large seizure of meth and guns. They’d raided the old Lucky 7 Pub. It was under new management, and the bikers had been usin’ the place for their meth distribution point. The guns were seized from a guy by the name of O’Mally.

“Looks like ya boy not just snitchin’ on us. You think O’Riley ratted the Irish out too?” Bang asked.

I shrugged. . .

Chapter 3

(DETECTIVE ABOTTS)

THE PUB . . .

Coats and I gathered all the evidence from the crime scene. O'Riley had become our prime informant on this case. He'd gotten Zaro locked up, and now proofre sat within our grasp. I looked O'Mally in the eyes as we walked him out of the pub in hand cuffs.

"We got you dead wrong. This time that Jewish son-of-a-bitch lawyer you got can't help you," I said cockily.

He chuckled as he walked. O'Mally resembled the Fighting Shamrock with a thick mustache curled and pointed at the tips. His muscular physique was threatening, but I paid it no mind, as I was winning this game right now—*even his top employee was on my payroll.*

I had O'Mally and his biker buddies backed against a wall. O'Mally was about to do a life bid because of O'Riley. We'd had the Irish on our radar for a while, but no one would testify or rat them out. Plus, all the witnesses ended up dead—*their throats slit with razor wire*.

I walked him to the police cruiser myself, then walked to my Impala and slid into the passenger seat, Coats waiting on me. I fastened the seat belt, then looked at him with a smirk.

"We finally got him."

Coats gave me a hearty handshake and a smile.

"What now?" he asked.

"Now we book his ass and keep O'Riley safe till the trial. His men are gonna try to kill him for sure," I replied.

"I already had him put in PC at the county jail. There's no way they gonna get to him," Coats said with confidence.

Coats and I rode to the police station, two happy men. We had been chasing the Irish mob for a while but were forced to stand down on the strength that they were rats. O'Riley was on our payroll, so we'd had to give him a pass—but not today. Today we were gonna celebrate for the team. This was a major win. Guns, drugs, meth . . . the bikers were just a consolation prize too.

I had O'Mally on the attempted murder of Coats and myself, as well as the murder of Marty. There was no way out for him now. I would make sure O'Riley was nowhere near him.

As we got to our desks, the chief walked in. His stomach hung over his waistline, and he wore a salt-and-peppered beard with a cheap suit and a body reeking of pork.

"I got new detail for you boys," he said.

We both shifted in our seats before he went on to explain how the Feds were putting together a new team in Rockford and they wanted me to head it. I smiled at the gesture, then continued putting the evidence into my log book.

Moments later, a woman stepped in wearing a *Purple Hills* black mini skirt with a white blouse—typical get-up for a woman in the FBI—and introduced herself as Shawnta Harris.

I shook her hand before the chief spoke again.

"Shawnta here is gonna be working with you and Coats. I need you guys to get out there and get some answers. There's a higher grade of heroin that's hit the city, and it's leavin' a lot of people in the morgue. It's rumored to be straight from Afghanistan, and I need you three to find out how these souped-up drugs made their way to *my* city."

After I shook Shawnta's hand, I looked over at Chief Wimberly, thinkin' he was born with that stressful look on his face. His brown tie never all the way tied.

"Chief, we're gonna make Shawnta feel like she been with us for years," I said, then stared at her.

Shawnta was a beautiful Black woman, resembling Maggie from *Chicago Med.* I pegged her to be about 55, though I knew a guy such as myself had no chance with her, so I had to admire her beauty from afar.

Coats didn't pay her the amount of attention I did, stayin' busy inventorying the evidence from the raid.

After the formalities were over, Chief Wimberly left us to get formally acquainted with our new co-worker. I asked her where she'd transferred from, as it was evident this wasn't her first time as a detective.

"Indiana," she replied and took a seat at the third vacant desk in the cubicle.

"This my desk?" she asked, not wantin' to be rude for her intruding.

"By all means, be my guest," I replied, holding my hand out to offer the seat.

She smiled and leaned back in the chair like she had been here for years.

"See, you get comfortable real quick," Coats said, walkin' over with a file in hand.

"Don't start no shit, please. Coats, play nice now," I interjected.

"I don't mean no harm, I'm just talkin'. Welcome to the team, Shawnta," he replied.

We talked a bit about Indiana, then offered her the opportunity to interrogate O'Mally. I wanted to see what type of skills she had when it came to good police work. She jumped at the opportunity.

Shawnta went in hard-nosed while O'Mally just stared her down like he was searchin' her face for some sort of weakness he could exploit. The more she talked, the more he just smiled, until he grew tired of her attempts to break him and leaned forward to yell, “Law-yer!”

He leaned back in his seat, relaxed.

Coats and I looked on from the one-way mirror with disgusted looks plastered on our faces. I shook my head. I didn’t need anything from O’Mally—he could just make the game over sooner. I had O’Riley, and that was good enough.

She walked out the room disappointed.

“Don’t look so gloom,” I said, though it was evident that she’d gotten discouraged by how the interview went.

I tried to convince her that everything would be fine and we already had the case in the bag.

She walked back to her desk and took a seat, so I asked what brought her to Rockford.

“My sister was DA here,” she answered.

“You mean to tell me your sister is Kimberly Yanzie?” I said with a sympathizing glare.

“That’s my family. I’m here to catch those bastards who did it,” she said, lettin’ her voice tail off like she was ashamed.

I tried to console her and said, “Your sister was a good DA. The only problem was she was married to the wrong guy.”

“She was married to a gang member, and he was the one who got her killed. So I won’t stop until I have them all in handcuffs,” she proclaimed outwardly.

And there it was—a woman with motive and driven by revenge. We had a good cop on our team. We were about to put the city into a clamp.

The story about Kim was she’d been killed by a terrorist over her boyfriend. It was all a big rumor mill inside the department, with nothing solid to go on. The only thing we had was some neighbors sayin’ they’d witnessed men with bow ties exiting her home. We got the same accounts when it came to Waaco, so the investigation was ongoing.

They were labeled terrorists because of the murder of the DA and the fact that there was a mass shooting in the projects—plus there was also the fact that one of the men yelled *Allahu Akbar* before the first shots were fired.

"So are you investigating her death while you're with us? If so, I'm here for you—whatever you need," I said with sincerity in my heart.

"I'm here for a lot of reasons," she said.

(ZAMAD)

Popeye and I walked the yard, discussing our plans to get the shipment of *fentanyl* to my people in Indiana. Jigs were running smoothly, and the hit they took for me was successful. I was glad to hear that everything was in play as we shook hands once our meeting was over before heading back to my unit.

Capo was at the poker table when I entered and ran straight over to me with a big broad smile.

"Guess what, big homie?" he said excitedly.

"What is it, my nigga?" I answered, irritated from the long walk.

"I'm 'bout to go home—immediate release," he remarked.

I searched his face for some sort of deception, though he wasn't really the type to play games. We walked to the cell, and he tried to explain how he'd got the enactment of some new fed law. I listened, wishing something like that would happen for me. I knew my time would come sooner than later though. I just had to be patient.

Later that night we sat talking.

"What are your plans once you get out?" I asked.

He looked at me cluelessly before shrugging his shoulders.

"Truthfully, I don't know, my nigga. I know I got a lot of time to make up for."

“That you do,” I said, then thought for a moment before asking if he and his crew would help my son in Rockford. Capo was loyal to me all thru his stay at Beaumont. I felt he was trustworthy. While Red’s people pressed everyone to get info on Red’s murder, he could easily have ratted me out for the money.

Capo would fit perfectly into my plans to get out of prison—I just needed to know if he would go along with what I’d planned. Right now though, Zaro needed his help. Thunder had been released from prison, and if I knew the nigga like I knew him, nothing would be safe. With his cousin Gambit being released too, they were devil’s spawn together.

“What you need me to do, big dawg?”

“I need you and ya boys to get with my son. You can make some real money in my city,” I said.

“Whatever you need, big dawg. Me and my niggas is at his disposal—and yours.”

“That’s good, ’cause I got some other shit I need you to handle for me.”

Capo sat up in his bed. He knew the conversation was about to get serious. I spoke in a hushed tone while I explained what I needed to get done. I was careful not to give it all to him at once. Though Capo’s loyalty to me was evident, some things had to be eased in. I couldn’t afford any missteps.

This was our last night together, so I stayed up all night, cramming his brain with my plans and how to handle my son. With Thunder and Gambit out of jail at the same time, I knew it would get volatile.

The morning came quick, with the sun beaming down into our window like the heavens had opened its gates for Capo’s release. They unlocked the doors, and I walked him up to R&D and gave him a hug. We promised to cross paths outside these walls, and he assured me—

"That situation with your son? Don't worry. Imma burn the city for him and free you 'til you free," he said.

It was an emotional moment for me—I almost wanted to cry.

We embraced each other for a second time, and I looked him in the eye.

"You all I got. Everything I told you is only for you. And no matter what happens, you die with that—that's all I ask of you. We forever indebted to each other," I said from the bottom of my heart.

He spun to walk off, and I watched his back as he passed through those double doors.

At once, a devilish grin slid onto my face . . .

(GAMBIT)

F.C.I. PEKIN

Walking through R&D after being gone for twelve years was a wonderful feeling. This day was long waited, as I passed through the lobby doors a free man—no probation, no halfway house, nothing.

Thunder was parked in front of the building, sitting inside his Track Hawk. I gawked at the car in awe; I'd only seen them in magazines, and now I was about to ride inside one.

Thunder hopped out, and we walked around each other in a circle, studying one another like two boxers sizing up their opposition. I dropped the manila envelope I was clutching, and we began to slap box.

The cops in the control booth must've thought we were serious because he yelled out, "Hey, you guys, cut that out!"

We both spun to look at him. Then Thunder slid his hand underneath his shirt. I knew what was about to come next, so I grabbed his arm.

"Hold up, fam, we good. Not now, not here," I said.

Thunder mugged the guard as he slid into the car.

"What's that nigga's name?" he asked.

I looked at the guy as we pulled off. “Colmen. Officer Thomas Colmen.”

I hated Colmen’s redneck ass to the core. He'd transferred from USP Thomson because he'd gotten caught up in a prison misconduct case for beating inmates. I guess him and a crew of COs were rumored to be beating inmates and all sorts of other shit. They shut the entire prison down because of it.

Thunder drove and gave me the update on what was going on while we were locked up. I shook my head at all the bullshit.

“I hated Kamar, and the fact he top dog out here . . . we definitely need to see about that,” I said.

Thunder was my big homie, and I trusted his lead. We were putting together a dynasty, so there’s expected to be some bumps in the road. It was better that I didn't have to worry about a P.O., because bodies were about to drop.

“You know this Kamar claiming he retired? I know it’s all bullshit though, ’cuz he got Zamad’s son out on top of shit—and the lil’ nigga in jail at that,” Thunder said.

“Zamad’s about to get his ass handed to him soon,” I proclaimed.

Thunder gave me a shocked look. “What you mean by that? What’s going on with him?”

“Word is he had something to do with Red getting killed. There’s no real proof, but the guys are investigating the situation. It's a cake in the oven on him as we speak,” I replied, as Thunder smirked.

“So is there a green light on him?” he asked, and I shook my head.

“That means we can put his son down with him. But what about Kamar? Is he in on this shit with Zamad? There’s no way his son got connections like he does so quickly,” Thunder said, brainstorming.

We were 30 minutes outside of Rockford, and there were a lot of moves that needed to be made. I was about to go see this nigga Kamar, and if he wasn't saying the right shit, I was prepared to leave him dead.

As Thunder parked the whip, he reached into the stash box. He handed me a Glock 23. I examined the fine piece of plastic and got stumped at the little box on the back of it.

Thunder chuckled. “It’s a switch. Turns the gun to a fully automatic.”

I guess these type of guns were common now—it wasn't like before we got locked up. I felt like Wesley Snipes in the movie *Demolition Man*, in search of the futuristic guns.

“This is Kamar’s spot,” Thunder said.

I nodded as he jacked the slide on his pipe. I did the same as we slid out the front of the Track Hawk.

I stood looking at an F-150 truck.

“The down payment on this truck is cheap,” came a voice from behind.

I spun to see a skinny white kid with a nice tailored suit on. I looked him up and down—he was well dressed, and his jewelry shimmered in the light.

This sight said one thing: Kamar was definitely in the game. He better say the right shit.

“Go get your boss, white boy,” I said aggressively.

“Ex-cuse me,” he stuttered, dragging his words out fearfully.

I stepped in his face, my expression like a hungry wolf. “You heard what the fuck I said. Now get the fuck outta here ’fore I start squeezing in this bitch,” I snarled.

He backed away, then trotted off.

Moments later, Kamar came out looking like he had just come from a video shoot.

I looked him up and down and smiled as we embraced each other with a half hug.

“Why you scaring my employees?” he said as we broke apart.

"We had to get your attention some type of way," I said, as he cut his eye over to Thunder, who was staring at him like a snake ready to strike.

Thunder and Kamar studied each other's gaze until I broke the eerie moment they were having.

"I see you doing good for yourself," I said, looking him over from head to toe.

He tried to playfully tuck his jewelry, which was his way of flexing. Thunder nodded behind me, his glare fixated on Kamar.

"Niggas saying you a million dollar nigga out here," I stated, waiting for his reaction.

He shook his head and rolled his eyes in Thunder's direction.

"Follow me to my office if your dawg don't mind," Kamar remarked.

I looked to Thunder. "I'll be back, fam. Imma talk to him for a minute."

We ducked off to the building as he led the way inside to his office.

He sat behind a large oak desk and opened a drawer. I thought he was going for a gun, so I touched my hip—until he pulled a cigar out, putting me at ease.

He smiled, and I knew he'd done that to see how fast I would be on the draw.

We talked for a while, and by the time I left his office, he'd given me the F-150 Thunder and I were looking at outside, plus hit my hand with some cash.

"I ain't got no dope, fam. I'm out the game on that note," he said.

I was glad Kamar did the right thing—because I'd planned on putting his ass down today if he didn't. This only spared him for the day, though. He still gotta answer about Flex.

"What's the word on Flex? You know who killed him?" I asked, looking him dead in the eye.

He shook his head. "Fuck, I been trying to figure that shit out myself so I could send my shooters."

I listened to him, then leaned back in my seat.

"You know anything about it? We got gang on standby in the city, and they want some answers on the big homie. Niggas feel like this your city, and you let this shit happen right under your nose," I replied, agitated.

"Calm down, my nigga, we gon' get to the bottom of this shit. Chill," he said, trying to defuse the situation.

I took a breath. I knew it was time for me to exit, as I'd got what I came for.

I stepped out the office and walked to the parking lot, where I told Thunder I would follow him to the hotel.

When we got to the hotel, Thunder questioned me on what Kamar and I talked about.

"Did he tell you anything about who killed Flex?" he asked anxiously, looking at me with a pleading gaze.

I shook my head. "He says he doesn't know anything, but I can tell he knows something."

"You should've smoked his ass right there," Thunder said coldly, then looked down at the money on the bed.

"How much is that?"

"It's a hunny bun," I replied.

He shrugged his face and sucked in a breath. "Psst, that's it? Outta all that time you did? Fam, I wanna kill that nigga."

"Easy, gang. We gon' get our time. Let his baby sleep. This shit chess, ain't checkers."

"Damn right. And now it's my move."

"What's the move?"

"I think we should wait till he throw that all-white party he has every year. The city gon' be there, and we can take them all out at one time," Thunder said.

I nodded, knowing it would be the perfect time.

It was rumored that Zaro was in jail, so it would be the perfect time to strike at Kamar. We could also find out who these bow-tie dudes is that everybody talkin' about.

Thunder had suspected Kamar strongly had something to do with Flex's death. Killing him out in the open like that wasn't a smart move. He was worth a lot more than just a revengeful murder. But Kamar was a sneaky, grimey dude—with him and Zamad pulling the strings with Zaro.

Thunder explained his plans to me, and I noted and listened attentively.

Thunder's phone buzzed before we heard a car door slam outside. He looked down at his phone and opened the door—

As Chubs walked in with his dreads over his face . . . two others stepped in behind him.

Chapter 4

(NYLON)

TWO WEEKS PRIOR . . .

Zoo and I hit the projects early Saturday mornin', same shit different day. Runnin' Concord was a full-time grind—no days off. We did our usual rounds, checkin' every corner, makin' sure niggas were on their job and not slackin'. This wasn't no game; we had eight buildings to keep locked down, and we patrolled the whole perimeter like hawks, eyes peeled for anything outta place. Ain't nobody really fucked with the back buildings though—they stayed empty for a reason. That's where we stashed the hammers—top-floor units, windows boarded, doors double bolted. Quiet, cold, and ready for war.

"We should give this place our own name," Zoo said.

I chuckled at the remark, but also knew he was right. "What should we call it?"

"I ain't gone cap, you niggas was drilling shit to get to where you at now; I would call it *Drill City*, especially if we make this bitch our own lil' city. Look around, my nigga, this a town within a city," he said, opening his arms as we walked.

We entered the last building where all our pipes were located. Zoo and I talked while we walked up the first flight of stairs until we noticed the door to Apt 6 was slightly ajar. Zoo and I looked at each other in unison. I put my index finger to my lips, shushing him before we pulled out our guns in sync.

We eased inside the apartment, creeping real slow with our guns drawn, in search of an intruder. It was hard to fathom someone had the balls to break into our shit like that, but Zoo and I went room to room nonetheless.

"Nylon, over here!" Zoo shouted as I ran toward him, gun at the ready to spark some shit up.

Zoo held some young-looking kid at gunpoint. The boy looked shook up and scared to death.

"This lil' nigga was in here sleeping," Zoo remarked as the boy stood there shaking like a two-dollar stripper.

"I'm sorry, you don't have to kill me. I didn't have no place to go, and my father brought me here before," he said.

"Fuck all that, you can't be breaking into people shit like that. I'd be wrong if I put a bullet in your head right now? You know where the pipes located—shit, you might be spying. I guess we gone have to run that shit across Zaro neem. They not gone be locked up for long," Zoo said.

"Anyway, how the fuck did you get in here?" I said, also holding him at gunpoint.

Zoo kept his gun to the boy's head too. This situation was getting sticky for him—he had to make all the right answers, or he was gone end up dead for sure.

Chapter 5

(KAMAR)

THE COLOSSEUM . . .

Chris and I stood in the middle of the Colosseum as he pointed out where the stripper poles would be placed. I wasn't paying him hardly any attention, as my mind was not in the game at the moment. The visit that Thunder and Gambit had paid me had me thinking; I didn't know what to expect from either of them, as they were both live wires.

Gambit and I had a past together, so I know he probably feels like I owe him, which is why I'd given him the F-150 and the lil' money. He was also my cousin. Thunder, on the other hand, was playing some other angle; he was a grimy nigga, and his whole demeanor was all about the fuckery. I felt he had something planned or in the works.

When they both first showed up, I thought Thunder and Gambit were here to avenge Flex's death, but the more I thought about it, the more it didn't fit. If that really was the case, Thunder was the type to shoot first and ask questions later, soo . . . I started to brainstorm other possible things Thunder would want until Chris brought me back to reality.

"Did you hear what I said?" Chris asked.

I shook the thought and then looked at him, trying to figure out what he'd originally said.

"What was that?" I asked before chuckling and smiling apologetically.

"Nothing, I just wanted to know where we would have the white tiger encaged?" he said excitedly.

I apologized for my lack of attention and let him finish getting things ready with the party planner. I walked out to the Bentley and sat in the passenger seat. After a few moments, I was lost scrolling on Instagram when a black Sprinter pulled up on the side of me. I immediately went for my pipe, but the side door opened too fast . . . it was full of dreadhead youngin's.

"Sup, Cuzzz!" one of the boys said, with a gun lying in his lap, long stick attached. I gripped my own Glock tightly, figuring if it was gonna pop off, they would've come up to my car already shooting. The boy looked down, realizing the disrespect that sat in his lap.

"Oh shit, my fault, homie. Are you Kamar?" he asked in a more calming tone.

I eased my finger from the trigger. "You must be Capo," I answered.

He popped out his van as I exited my Bentley in unison, and we met each other in front of the Bentley.

"This a nice ride. 2023! Shitt," he stated whilst looking it over, nodding in approval.

"Yeah, got that big boy Hellafant under the hood. Zamad say yawl ready to put in some work," I said, getting straight to the point.

"Yeah, we were cellies in—"

I cut his sentence short. "No disrespect to you or the time yo spent in that mufucka, but I like to concentrate on what goin' on out here in the free world. I love the nigga Zama to deff, but we in two different places; you wit' me now."

"I can dig that. So what's the deal, cuz?"

"First off, chill with the *cuz* shit. You in Drill City, fam. Ain't no Bloods or Crips this way, ya feel me?"

Capo nodded attentively as I spoke. I gave him the layout on how shit worked and let him know that he'd be assisting the youngin', Nylon.

After talking with him for some time, Chris and the party planners were finally done. Chris slid into the front seat, and I told Capo to follow us—I was gonna take him to the projects to meet Nylon.

We drove out to the old Waaco, now known as Drill City. I pulled up to the building where Nylon normally hung out and whipped into the parking lot. Nylon stepped out with Zoo right behind him as Capo's driver pulled in next to me in a Sprinter van. We all slid out in unison, and Zoo and Nylon met us at the front of my Bentley. I introduced them, and we all slapped hands.

"Where you from again?" Zoo asked.

"We Hellraiser Crips, cuz," Capo replied, stepping close to Zoo, adding some emphasis. He looked Zoo up and down as if he wanted smoke.

Zoo touched his hip suddenly while Capo's people drew their guns with lightning speed. Nylon and Zoo up'd their poles on cue as Kamar eased off the hood of his car and got between Zoo and Capo.

"Whoa, you niggas need to chill out. This ain't what yawl here for."

Zoo had murder in his eyes. Capo looked over to Kamar, who had pleading eyes.

"Cuz, what you trying to do? Check my chain or some? This ain't that, cuz," Capo said, looking to Zoo then to me.

"Ya man need to dead that extra shit. All that aggressive shit we can do without—it ain't called for," Zoo said.

"Yawl niggas lower them guns. We all on the same team," I repeated and gazed at everybody's face.

It took a few minutes to squash the beef between Zoo and Capo, but they eventually shook hands. He introduced his people—four of them here in the Sprinter, with six of them all together.

"My two lil' twins, R1 and R2, are on their way with the chops and sticks," Capo said.

"That's good, 'cause we got some shit to do. Yawl can stay in the back building. It's like six apartments, and you can have any one," Nylon said.

I could tell Capo was amazed at what he was seeing.

"Yawl own all this shit?" he asked.

"Something like that. We got to get some things straight with the mayor and city, but we'll have it soon enough," Kamar interjected.

Capo looked around and nodded. "This is cool."

"Best part, the cops don't come out here," Zoo remarked.

I looked at Zoo and could see he still had some malice in his heart. He and Capo were gonna be a problem to be around each other.

After the meet and greet, Nylon led them to where they would stay, while Chris and I got back onto the highway—we had some business to handle in Chicago.

(O'RILEY)

COUNTY JAIL...

C/O Wiggins led me to the chassis factory.

"How long do you think you'll be here today?" he asked as we passed the regular units.

I always got paranoid about someone seeing me and trying to get up on me with a makeshift prison knife. I don't think Wiggins would let that happen though, as he was a hard-nosed C/O who didn't like nobody. I felt safe with him.

"Hopefully this will be my last day in jail, so I'm going to give it all I got today," I replied.

Wiggins replied with a chuckle.

We made it to the room—Coats and Abotts were there waiting on me. When I stepped inside, there was an open pad lying on the table with a pen. I glanced down at it before taking my seat. I scanned the paperwork in the hope they were my release papers.

“We got good news and bad news,” Abotts said, looking me hard in the eye.

“Okay, give it to me,” I replied and leaned back.

“We got O'Mally. The case isn't really solid, so you're going to have to take the stand on him,” Coats said.

I took a deep breath and shook my head as he dropped me with another bombshell.

“The evidence on the kid Zaro is shaky at best. Is there any way you can help us find the gun that he shot the girl with?” Abotts said.

“How am I supposed to do that?”

“What if we put you in the unit with him?”

I looked at him sideways. *Is this guy fucking serious?* I thought to myself. I almost choked on my own laughter—this guy was really trying to get me killed. From that point on, I thought it was all a setup.

“Are you two clowns getting high off that dope you're finding or what? Them fucking nigga sons of bitches would kill me just for being white, let alone getting info from them. Can't do it,” I said sternly while shaking my head.

This funny mutha-fucker had the balls to start laughing. I wanted to wrap my hands around his fat neck and crush his skull in. He knew that I needed him, that he had me boxed in, that I was at their mercy.

Coats was always quiet, and it made me feel like there was more than meets the eye with him.

“Are you guys gonna get me out of here today? I did my part. O'Mally's in jail. You got the kid on the bank robbery—you got to let me go before they get to me.”

Coats leaned forward.

“Relax. We got your paperwork right here. We're gonna send you to Colorado to hide out till O'Mally's trial starts. We do need you to get Zaro to talk some type of way,” Coats said, a very serious Michael Myers–made psychotic look on his face.

I had to think for a minute. Was it possible for me to pull off? He did still owe me for the guns, and maybe—just maybe—he hadn't heard I was a rat.

I honestly didn't think anyone knew for sure, but stress wasn't the court of law. You don't need to go beyond reasonable doubt when it comes to the law of the land. It's shoot first and ask questions later out here, even for mere assumptions.

"I'll see what I can do once I'm out of here. I'll request the money that he owes me," I replied.

Coats and Abotts looked at each other and nodded in unison.

As I walked back to the unit with Wiggins, I was thinking about writing Zaro a kite and sending it to him.

How would I find him though?

I got back to the pod and walked into the cell while Ralph was reading a book. He laid it on his chest.

"What happened? Are you going to get out?" he asked.

"You can bet your last dollar on that," I said with a wide grin.

"That's great! When are you leaving? Were you able to do the same with me like you said?"

I didn't know how to respond to his question. Abotts never mentioned anything about Ralph. In fact, he was just the backup in case one of them decided to take it to trial. I didn't want to lie. I really tried to help him out—he'd been a good friend since we've been in jail. I only wanted him to follow me so I wouldn't get stuck with a bad cellie.

"I'll do what I can to help you get out of here once I'm free."

I studied his face for some sort of reaction, but he gave me an odd, demonic gaze with a devilish smirk. He eased towards me, his massive frame blocking any type of path I may have had to the door.

As he dug into his underwear, my eyes widened at the sight.

(O'MALLY)

FEDERAL HOLDING . . .

I paced back and forth in my pod while I anxiously waited for my attorney to show up. Bruiser and Steve were on the upper level looking down on me. We all were in this bind together—all in a bind because of O'Riley.

The feds thought they could get him to rat us all out and that we wouldn't figure it out. I'd been onto his and Marty's shit for some time now, and God, did I want to kill them both myself, but the plan was to get them to take each other out.

I should've did O'Riley in when I had the chance. Now we were all paying the ticket.

Bruiser walked down the steps looking like he was about to come out and say something stupid.

"When is your lawyer guy gonna get us outta here?" he said in his southern raspy biker tone.

"Calm down. I got this under control. This type of shit don't happen overnight though, you'll have to be patient," I replied, trying to calm him down.

Bruiser was overly animated, his attitude showing as he shook his head angrily. Steve walked up shortly after, his face also balled up. I looked them both over with a scolding gaze.

"Your rat buddies is the reason we're in here now," he said. "Fuck! I knew better than to deal with any of you guys. You're all fucking rats!"

If I wasn't before, I was at the boiling point now. I lunged at his throat like a venomous snake attacking its prey. I grabbed him by his fat neck and pressed my thumb hard into his collarbone, backing him into the wall.

Bruiser saw Steve in my grasp and came over to help him. I knocked him to the ground with a right hook before grabbing Bruiser's throat. I looked him in the eyes as he gagged and gasped for air while I tried to squeeze the life out of him like a python would.

“Listen close, you fucking punk. I should cut your fucking tongue out and use it to wipe O'Riley's snitch ass with. If you ever put my name in the same sentence as a fucking rat, I will kill you—then your entire family. You got that?” I said with menacing eyes.

His eyes began to roll into the back of his head, so I shook him like a rag doll.

“Say something, you prick. Did you hear me?” I repeated.

He nodded, so I let him go, collapsing into a puddle on the ground.

My stomach started to rumble—it was already past noon and I hadn't had anything to eat.

“Go get me a soup, you fat slob,” I ordered Bruiser.

Steve slowly came to on the floor while the whole unit watched in suspense, trying to act normal.

I looked their way angrily. “What are all you pussies gawking at?”

Bruiser helped Steve up, and they both walked away while I went to watch SportsCenter on the TV. Nobody wanted to question me about anything.

Moments later, Bruiser returned with a soup in his hand.

“Go make it,” I said, and he trotted off.

Bruiser brought this on himself, and I don't tolerate disrespect from anyone—so he got lucky.

While in front of the TV, my name was called. I looked up at Bruiser. Him and Steve stood looking down on me with daggers in their eyes.

“O'Mally, your attorney's here,” he shouted out while I buttoned my jumpsuit.

Wiggins led me out the pod to the glass attorney/inmate room—glass for easy viewing by the cops.

Frank Vela was the highest-paid lawyer in the city. He dressed the part, so hopefully he played the part too and came with some good news.

He held his hand out for me to shake, and I just stared at it like it had shit on it.

"Why the fuck am I still here?" I stated.

"These types of things take time. I can't just get you out of here because you ordered it."

Frank was lucky I couldn't put hands on him, because I wanted to mug him so hard as I took my seat.

Frank and I had a long-standing relationship in which I learned he was a conniving Jew. Frank played my friend Kelogg out of 150 thousand dollars. I held that over his head, knowing in time I would make sure that Jew prick's only breaths were in an oxygen tank.

Frank had a bad gambling habit, and he'd lost a lot of money in Vegas. This was part of his personality that only his clients could see.

Frank's retainer might've been excessive, but to me it was free.

The only reason Frank was still alive was his political connections. He had dirt on the city's most prominent figures. It's how he got the most notorious criminals off with mounds of evidence against them. His knowledge of self-preservation is the only thing that really kept him alive.

"Why the fuck am I still in jail?" I spat, looking at him with narrowing eyes.

He brushed the length of his suit before speaking.

"This thing isn't as clean cut as you think. O'Riley went all the way with it. The cops that are on your case are straight-up, so I'm trying to come up with a different approach."

My gaze pierced his soul, and I could tell this fool was lying. I could smell the fear all over him.

"You reek of fear. Get my paperwork together. I expect to be out next week."

"That's not possible. I'm gonna have to get you in court, and your court date is next month. You're asking me to promise something that's out of my reach," he pleaded.

But I rose from my seat, letting the C/O know I was done here. Wiggins stepped to the glass door, and I looked back at Vela with an icy stare.

"You got one week," I said, as I exited the room, leaving him sitting there alone.

(FRANK VELA)

I sat shooting daggers into O'Mally's back with my eyes. He was the textbook bully, and I regretted ever going into business with the dude.

As the C/O returned, my thoughts were on how O'Mally would get what he had coming. I was fed up. There was no way I was going to keep accepting his bullshit—I had to get him out the way, and I had just the plan for him.

"You got anyone else you need to speak to?" the C/O said, shaking me from my ruminations.

I looked into my day planner. "Uhm, yes. Can you get me Zaro Gates, please?"

The C/O nodded, then trotted off. I flipped through Zaro's file and looked over the papers before Zaro walked in. I stood to shake his hand as he entered.

I leaned back in my seat and unbuttoned my blazer jacket comfortably. I felt relaxed now. Being around O'Mally was like sitting on the edge of a razor.

"I'm good and ready to get out of here. Any good news for us?" Zaro asked.

"As a matter of fact, yes. Your judge is Pearson, right?" I asked, Zaro nodding in response.

"Got a way to get the whole case thrown out. It's not guaranteed though, and it's gonna cost," I said with a serious look on my face.

He sat straight up in his seat. "Money ain't an issue, Frank. I already gave you 100 G's and I'm still in jail. Shoot the price, open the gates, and get me and my niggas outta here! What's it gonna cost?"

I scribbled on a notepad, ripped the paper off the top, folded it, and slid it to him.

"Keep that safe till you get to your pod," I said and winked at him while rising from my seat, signaling to the guard our visit was up.

The guard came to get Zaro and led him out. I knew exactly how I was going to play this situation out—with only one outlier: the murder case on Zaro, which is proving to be much harder to get dropped.

(SAVON)

I looked in the mirror as I prepared for my visit. Zaro and I had been together for at least two months now, with Cowboy still not knowing. I was having problems dealing with this whole thing, especially since my best friend was dead.

I hadn't really thought too much of her death because I'd been preoccupied with Zaro smothering me with love.

It was really hard for me when I found out they were charging him with Tif's murder. I knew it was a load of shit, but so much drama was going on it was starting to become unbearable. I had to focus on the good things in my life—like Zaro and the fact I had my brother back.

I put the final touches on my hair and looked in the mirror. I hadn't seen him in two weeks, as the jail went on lockdown during my last attempt, so I was happy to see him now.

I slid my car into gear and adjusted the rearview mirror, noting an unmarked car pull behind me and block my path out.

"Ugh, what the hell do they want?" I muttered. Cowboy wasn't here, so they should just be in and out.

The guy walked around to my window and I slid the window down.

"Can I help you with something? You're blocking my path," I said, irritated. I had to get to my visit in 30 minutes.

"My name is Detective Shawnta Lawry. Can you step out of the vehicle, please?" she asked in an authoritative tone.

I frowned, wondering what she wanted with me.

"What's this about?"

"We need you to come downtown with us. I'll explain once we're there."

I shook my head. *This could not be happening to me right now.*

"I'm kind of busy right now," I replied, agitated.

"Miss, you don't have an option," she said, then proceeded to open my door.

Shawnta seemed like a real GI Jane type. She had short dreads, skin as black as coffee, and she wore no makeup whatsoever.

Her appearance was akin to the Wicked Witch of the West.

I stepped out the car and she walked me to the back of her vehicle. Two squad cars accompanied her as I was escorted downtown.

The police interrogation rooms were small. I felt boxed in and confined, which caused my anxiety to act up. I sat in the chair on edge—every little noise had me at attention as I sat there for almost an hour.

Finally, they brought me snacks, but still no one had come to tell me why I was even here. It was driving me nuts.

Suddenly the doorknob twisted and Shawnta was back. She walked around the table and took a seat. She began to get herself comfortable, making me wait further still in anticipation.

I looked at her anxiously, scouting for a sign of what this was even about.

She opened the folder and slid me a picture of a mutilated body.

"Recognize that person?" she said somberly.

I turned my head at the sight—it was *grotesque*.

I shook my head, almost ready to throw up.

“Of course you don't. This is the leftovers of your dead friend Ms. Tifanny,” she replied, then pulled another photo from the folder. “You know who this is, don't you?” she asked.

I didn't know how to answer the question. I'd seen this play out all the time on *First 48* though—they'd play the good cop, bad cop role, and I was sure there were two other cops monitoring the entire interrogation.

I said the only thing I could think of without getting myself in a clam.

“Lawyer!”

She looked at me with a confused glare.

“Your boyfriend killed your best friend and—”

I cut her off before she could finish.

“Am I under arrest?” I asked sharply.

“Not at the moment. But that doesn't mean you won't be later . . .”

“Can I call myself a ride, please?”

She searched my face for some sort of sympathy. Suddenly the doorknob twisted again. A detective walked in and Shawnta glared up at him.

“She lawyered up on me first round,” she remarked as the male officer peered at me.

“I'm Detective Coats. You're in a lot of trouble, young lady. Do you want us to pin this murder on you? Because you're gonna go down for this,” he said angrily.

This must be the bad-cop routine. The whole First 48 scene was playing out in front of me.

“I already asked for an attorney once. Can you please handle that for me?” I asked, frustrated and ready to go.

They both scoffed, and I could tell neither of them was happy. As they were about to exit the room, Shawnta spoke.

“The next time you see me, I'll be putting these silver bracelets on you—and won't be giving you the option to get out of jail free. You oughta be ashamed of sleeping with a murderer,” she said and chuckled on her way out the door.

I was left to think about everything. I just couldn't believe Zaro had killed Tifanny. I'd known him since he was young, and Zaro didn't come off as the type.

He had no reason to murder her either. Tifanny and I were close, and Zaro knew that. They had to have the wrong person.

I thought about how Zaro had come to her funeral and remembered him even consoling me . . . there was no way he had anything to do with this.

I called Zaro's Aunt Sheila to come pick me up from the precinct.

As we drove, Sheila headed instinctually toward the projects. I'd forgotten she didn't know I moved. She looked over at me, noticing the stress painted broadly all over my face.

"You still stay out in Concord?" she asked, breaking the silence in the car.

"I don't live in the PJs anymore, Ms. Sheila," I stated.

She smiled at me. "Oh, I'm sorry, honey, I didn't know. How about you and I catch some dinner? I'll make some fish. It looks like you need someone to talk to."

"Is it that obvious?" I asked, and she chuckled.

"It's alright, honey. I'll cook some dinner and we'll talk about it."

We talked about my friend Tif and her death. It was the first time I'd spoke on it.

Tears welled in my eyes as we talked, but Sheila promised me everything would be okay and that Zaro would've never done something like that.

I trusted Ms. Sheila—she was a very wise Christian woman.

It was too late to visit with Zaro, so I agreed to spend the night at Sheila's house. Maybe I could get some peace of mind there.

We made a quick stop at Logi on North Main St., and she gave me a short list of items that were needed with her Link card.

I slid out the car as Sheila complained of a leg problem, so I just left her in the car. The sun had set, and it was dark out now.

I looked back to the car.

"You gonna be alright?"

"I'll be fine. Just don't take too long—I want to watch *Love After Lockup*," she said.

I chuckled, then shut the door.

Vrm, vrm, vrm—my phone buzzed as I walked through the sliding doors. It was Zaro.

I had already anticipated his call after I hadn't shown up for the visit.

I walked around the market while cradling the phone to my ear. Our conversation kept me busy while I went down the list of items we needed for the night.

Our relationship was really starting to bloom into a special one. It was obvious through everyone's eyes that I was in love with him.

I was sure he felt the same way, which is why I couldn't believe he would kill Tifanny.

I honestly thought the police wanted to frame him and played on my emotions to do it. I didn't fall for the okey-doke, but I still really wanted to ask him if it was true.

I didn't want to ruin the moment though, as we'd started out talking about why I didn't visit and quickly went to another topic. He didn't feel comfortable with it—and I didn't either.

I did tell him there was one final step in completing our love for each other though.

He chuckled. "What's that?"

"We have to tell my brother. I think it's time we told him," I replied.

The line went silent.

I heard him take a deep breath.

"Yeah, I know—eventually. I just don't want him to take it the wrong way. You know how Cowboy is . . . just let me be the one to tell him, please."

"Okay, but let's not drag this out," I said, stepping out into the parking lot.

He ended the call abruptly as I got to the car, and I just started putting the bags into the back seat.

As I slid into the passenger seat, I realized I was so busy talking to Zaro and loading the bags that I hadn't even noticed Sheila wasn't in the car.

I looked around, wondering what was happening—she was too old to be playing games like this.

I stepped out the car and scanned the area, when I noticed a car was running with the driver's door left ajar.

My mind was all over the place. I didn't know what to think, so I dialed her number.

Vrm, vrm, vrm, vrm.

I heard a phone buzzing between the seats and fished it out. The caller tag was from me.

Where was she? Why was her phone left behind?

"Dammit!" I muttered.

(COWBOY)

Sittin' in my sister's old spot had my stomach twisted. That apartment reeked of bad memories, ghosts I thought I left buried. I never planned on touchin' this life again, but I let Nylon talk slick and pressure me back in.

Now here we was—just left the meet with Ackmed for the re-up.

Zaro been eatin' heavy while I was down. Nigga was really gettin' to it. We dropped half a mil on Ackmed like it was nothin'. If you told me a year ago I'd be movin' work like this, I would've laughed in your face. But here I was—

this *his* plan from the jump. Just didn't include me layin' in a hospital bed, half-dead, tryna remember my name.

Shit changed after I took them shots. I changed.

But not enough to stay out.

Now I'm sittin' in a dusty-ass stash spot with five bricks of dogfood laid out like trophies.

Vrm, vrm, vrm.

Phone buzzed. It was Rene—said they ready to start cookin' this new batch of D.

I got up off that sunken-ass couch and grabbed the duffle with two keys of raw Afghan heroin. That heavy, uncut shit.

I stepped out the shake house in the back, night air hittin' my face like cold steel. I scanned the block as I came out the building—habit.

All the homies was posted at the front gates, where the only way in or out was. Just how we liked it.

Controlled. Watched.

Then I heard it—*rustle*. Leaves shiftin' on the side of the yard.

I froze.

Every little sound got me on edge these days.

Didn't think twice. I reached under my hoodie, wrapped my fingers 'round the grip. Pulled the steel halfway out the holster, thumb on the safety.

I been hit once. Never again.

"I must be trippin'," I muttered, head low, eyes cuttin' corners while I moved toward the shake spot.

As I walked, a lil' kid slid up outta the shadows—it was 2 a.m. in the trap.

What the fuck this lil' bad-ass doin' out here this late? I thought.

Then they popped out. Both of 'em. Dracos in their hands, muzzles flashin'.

Daaadaaaaaaaaaow! Daaadaaaaaaaaaow!

The night split open with gunfire.

I stumbled back, heart jumpin' out my chest, Glock already comin' up in my hand.

Boc! Boc! Boc! Boc! Boc! Boc! Boc!

Shells popped, smoke in the air, muzzle flames dancing. My Glock moving between shadows, back and forth, just pulling—no thinking, just instincts.

More shots cracked off from deeper in the cut. Couldn't even tell where they coming from.

I dove behind a car, breath heavy, ears ringing, eyes flicking in the dark. The two lil' boys still letting it rip—wild, reckless, rounds smashing metal and glass.

Darkness had my vision locked, couldn't see nothing but flickers in my peripheral.

I caught a shadow moving—didn't care who the fuck it was.

I raised the Glock, squeezed off. *Pop! Pop! Pop!*

The shadow dropped.

Then I felt it—hot, sharp pain tearing through my leg.

"Ahhh, shit!"

It was copious—Blood . . . warm . . . running down my jeans, my heart pounding like a drum.

I yelped, pain shooting up my leg. *This shit can't be real,* I thought. I had to get the fuck up out this spot.

A high-pitched whine cut through the night. I looked up—two lil' shooters jumpin' on the back of some four-wheelers. They peeled off down the hill—the only way out, bullets still barking as they dipped from the projects, brass hittin' concrete.

I popped up, squeezed at the bikes—*boc! boc! boc! boc! boc!*

I kept dumpin' till the clip ran dry.

Then Zoo came flying round the corner, F&N in his hands with the switch on it. The sound was crazy—like a chopper touching down—bullets slicing the night air.

Fi! Fi! Fi! Fi! Fi! Fi! Fi!

I spun, eyes darting for the duffle with the kilos . . .

It was gone.

"FUCK!" I cursed angrily as Zoo walked up.

"What's good, my baby? You a'ight?" he asked.

"They got the dope," I answered. My adrenaline was goin', so I couldn't even feel the gunshot wound until Zoo and I got to the apartment and he noticed the blood.

"Damn, bro, you got hit in the ass," he said, looking at the wound.

"Damn. Does it look bad?" I asked, somewhat angrily.

I shook my head, hopin' I didn't have to go to the hospital. If Crystal found out, she'd be pissed—I told her I was done with this life.

"It don't look bad, but I bet you feel like an ass," Zoo said, joking while laughing.

"This shit serious, nigga. They took the dope."

He suddenly went serious. "Damn, Nylon ain't gon' like this."

Just as he said it, Nylon walked in with Capo in tow. They all had high-powered rifles in their hands and looked like they was about to go to war. Capo stood militant with his gun out.

"What the fuck just happened?!" Nylon asked, his gaze murderous.

"We gotta get Cowboy to the hospital," Zoo interjected.

Nylon looked at me sympathetically. "You a'ight? Where you hit at?" he asked, concerned.

"In the ass. I'm good, fam. Shit felt like it went in and out. I don't need to get to the hospital—it's just startin' to burn."

Everyone chuckled, knowin' I was fine.

"Okay, I'll take you myself. What about the work?" Nylon asked.

I dropped my head shamefully. "I dropped the bag, and one of them niggas must've picked it up during the commotion of the shootout."

"Fuck! Zaro gon' be pissed when he finds out you lost the bag. That was the first re-up from Ackmed," he ranted.

"Fam, we need to do somethin' about this wound," I said.

I limped toward the door, Nylon leadin' the way.

"I lost three kilos. There's still two more in the stash," I said and winced as I slid into the front seat of the Hellcat.

"Man, get a towel or somethin'. I don't want your bloody ass leakin' on my seat," he said. I took my shirt off and sat on it as we rode toward the hospital.

I noticed he was headin' toward Rockford Memorial, so I spoke up.

"Don't go to Rockford. I don't want Crystal to find out I got shot."

Nylon erupted in laughter, the car swervin' as he busted a gut.

"Nigga, she gon' know somethin' happened when they put yo ass in a sling."

"Whatever, nigga. Just take me to Swedson on the east side."

Nylon's demeanor switched in a split second as he turned his gaze to me seriously.

"We gotta figure somethin' out about this work. Them Arabs gon' be callin' about that bread soon," Nylon said nervously before scoffin' and shakin' his head.

"It'll be a'ight. They didn't get everything," I replied.

"These niggas ain't got no type of understanding, you feel? These the same mufuckas that took Flex 'nem out," Nylon spoke, a slight fear in his voice.

His gaze was pure terror. "You talkin' about them bowtie killas everybody been talkin' about?"

He nodded slow. "Yeah, that's them."

As we pulled up to the ER doors of Sweds, I saw my sister standin' at the nurse's station. I wondered what she was doin' there as I slid out the car, but she shot me a concerned glare as I limped inside.

"What happened to you?" she asked, disdain in her voice.

I was ashamed to tell her I'd been shot again, but the look on my face said it all.

"Never mind. Don't answer that. At least you look ok."

"What about you?" I asked.

"I think Sheila may have been kidnapped, so I'm checkin' all the hospitals to be sure."

Nylon's face scrunched up, and we both shifted our gaze at each other.

"What? Do you guys know somethin'?" Savon asked anxiously, her concern for Sheila obvious.

"We just had a shootout in the projects. This shit might all be related," Nylon said before diggin' his phone out.

Zaro ain't gon' take this shit well, I thought to myself as Savon began to tell me what happened at the grocery store.

I was piecin' it all together when Nylon barked orders into his phone and turned to me.

"You gon' be good with sis? I gotta make some moves before the Arabs find out about the shootout, and we gotta find Aunt Sheila," he snapped.

I nodded. "Yeah, I'm good, fam," I answered.

Savon helped me to the back, and Nylon dipped out in a hurry.

I was curious why Savon would jump straight to a kidnapping conclusion, so I planned to ask her about it after the doctors finished dressin' my wound.

HOURS LATER . . .

Savon and I rode home in Ms. Sheila's Impala.

"Before I forget," she said, diggin' into her Gucci handbag and handin' me a piece of paper.

"This a ransom note," I said.

"That's what they left behind."

I sat in deep thought, about to call Nylon and let him know, when suddenly my Instagram chimed.

A video had been posted. I opened it . . .

There was Zaro's Aunt Sheila, sittin' in a chair, zip-tied. Three young lookin' dudes circled around her. Looked like they were inside a vacant building. She had a gun to her head and her face was drenched with tears.

I felt so much sympathy for her.

"Ahaa! We got somebody aunty. Come with ten bricks . . . of raw, that is—and you might get this old bitch back alive," one of the gunmen said viciously.

"Nawe, G. Let's fuck this blackberry," another shooter said, grabbin' his crotch.

This was all bad.

Savon looked at the video, appalled. She shook her head. "This is unbelievable."

I rubbed her back as she cried in the driveway, sobbin' loud.

"We'll get her back," I tried to say in the most comfortin' tone.

After twenty minutes of tryna console Savon—who was badly shaken up—I was finally able to calm her.

We stepped into the house, and I went straight to my room to change clothes. Sheila was family too. She pretty much raised me after my mama died.

There had to be somethin' we could do to get her back. But ten kilos? That was a heavy-ass order.

On top of that . . . I didn't even know who we was up against.

Vrm, vrm, vrm. My phone buzzed. It was Nylon.

"What's up, gang," I answered.

"Yo, this shit bad. Gang niggas just sent a video to my IG—some niggas out the Raq snatched up Aunt Sheila," Nylon said, irate.

"I seen it. Niggas sent me the same video. But how you know they outta Chicago? Is they the same ones that shot up the projects?" I asked.

"I'm sure it is. Zaro can't pay the ticket on that ransom—ten bricks is a lot. We ain't got it right now unless Kamar steps in."

"Have you talked to him?" I asked.

"Check it out, look, I'm 'bout to pull up on you. Can you put in some work?" he asked.

"I'm at my place," I said, then ended the call. I walked to my closet and grabbed my vest and twin Glock 19s with the switch. I popped in the 30 sticks and exited the room with murder on my mind. All that church boy shit was out the window for now. Crystal would just have to understand this wasn't business, it was personal. Niggas pushing us to the limit, and it was time to load up. I missed the first war because of the coma, so I'm not missing this one.

When I walked into the living room, Crystal surprised me—she was sittin' with Savon. Her eyes were wet when she looked up at me, and the gun in my waistband spoke for me.

Her eyes shifted from my stick to the vest before she spoke, "You just got shot, baby. You shouldn't be in the streets."

"I got to do what's best for gang, baby. Either you wit' me, or you against me."

She rose from her seat to hug me. "Promise me you won't do this forever, and I'll wait for you."

It made me feel really good knowin' she wasn't gon' leave me.

"I promise, baby," I said, and we hugged.

Vrm, vrm, vrm. My phone buzzed. That meant Nylon was here. I looked at the tag—unknown caller. I stepped onto my porch and answered the phone as Nylon drove up in a Striker, Zoo already in the back seat. The line was silent . . .

Then someone spoke.

"This bitch 'bout to be dead. You niggas need to come up with that dope," they hissed.

I couldn't help but think the voice sounded familiar—it was almost like someone had come back from the dead.

"You don't have to do this, my nigga. We ain't got the money you think we got," I said, pleading for Sheila's return without the violence. I knew it would be fruitless, though; I just had to try.

I heard a snicker on the other end as I cradled the phone to my ear, slidin' into the front seat of the Striker.

"Who is that?" Nylon whispered. I shrugged, then put the phone on speaker so he could hear the convo.

"Look, my nigga, yawl got that work you took from my homie, and we need that back, so don't play with me."

Nylon whipped his head towards the phone after hearing him talk. His face was in total shock.

"Calico, we know that pussy-ass nigga," Nylon said. I frowned when he said that—now I was really pissed. Calico was there the night I got put in that coma.

"Just have that dope by tomorrow, or this bitch dead. Yawl got 24 hours. I'll call back later with instructions," he spat, then ended the call.

I looked to Nylon for an answer. "So what now?"

He shook his head. I knew this wasn't about the dope either. They were gonna kill Aunt Sheila anyway. There was no doubt in my mind about that, seein' as they think we were the ones who killed Flex. I knew nothing about Calico and the whole situation really, 'cause I was in a coma, but the family was ready as we drove down West State Street. Zoo clutched the AR-15 in the back seat, lookin' at everything movin' as we drove to nowhere in particular. We were lookin' for any target to hit at this point.

"Think we should holler at Kamar to help us?" I asked.

"We'll get at him later," Nylon said.

Chapter 6

(KAMAR)

I sat in my office, watchin' the large screen. There was breakin' news on the city's latest violence as the anchor reported about a shootout in the projects. It made me sit on the edge of my seat, as I automatically thought about Switch Gang Family. Even though I knew they could definitely handle their own, I knew this was bad for business. Ackmed had just put 5 kilos of raw on them, and he wasn't the type of guy to play about his money. He'd come straight from the Middle East only to sell Afghan heroin. Saleen had placed him there just for that sole purpose. I peered out the window to the parking lot and watched an F-150 pull up.

"Fuck do he want?" I muttered as I opened my top desk drawer and grabbed my Glock 23. I tucked it into the small of my back as I got to my feet and took a deep breath before heading out the door to handle the situation. Gambit may have been family, but his loyalty was to Thunder and the Wolf Pack.

As Thunder hopped out the truck, I noticed who he had with him. I squinted my eyes just to be sure it was really him.

"This can't be, I thought that nigga was dead," I uttered as I walked to the lobby area.

Chris Wiggins sat at his desk, lookin' over some papers.

"What can I do for yawl today?" I asked Thunder.

"You can start by cuttin' us in on this piece-of-shit business you runnin'. I want 50 percent of whatever you make per month, and I definitely need 60 percent of that party," he spoke with venom.

I looked over his shoulder to see a Sprinter van pull up and counted four other shooters, all strapped, hop out the van. I chuckled at his audacity.

"So, this is an extortion move. Nigga, do you know the pull I got? You might want to check yo lil' hyenas and let 'em know what they really signed up for. You don't wanna go to war with me," I said, easing my hand to my gun.

Calico drew his Glock and pointed it in my direction first. "You don't wanna do that, Big Dogg," he said, ready to spark.

I shook my head. "So this is what it's come to? You ain't gotta do this."

He laughed demonically. "You started this shit. Who killed Flex?"

A lump formed in my throat, makin' it hard for me to swallow. My palms had begun to sweat, which was unusual for me. I glanced at Calico, his finger wantin' to curl that trigger bad, and was speechless.

"You just had all the rap, now you quiet. Don't think I don't know what happened. You and Zamad's son helped them Al-Qaeda mufukas murk Flex. That shit got your name all over it," Thunder spat.

His version of what happened was precise and hard for me to deny. My mind pondered how he'd known, so I wasn't sure if it would be wise to even offer any denial—that might be taken as an insult. Flex had brought it all on himself by robbing and killing Shareef, but my mind was at odds over my next move, as Thunder was very unstable right now. The odds of him blowing up were very high, and I felt lying would only add insult to injury.

I dropped my head then scoffed. "I never killed a man that didn't deserve it. Flex brought death to his doorstep."

I said this somberly in hopes he would show some empathy, but his face just twisted up.

"You really testin' my patience right now," he replied before shifting his sight to Calico. Thunder marched toward me and reached for my wrist, tugging at my diamond-crusted Patek.

"This outta suffice for the time being," he spat.

I stared at him, stunned at what was transpiring. He snaked his hand toward my back, confiscated my glizzy, and popped the clip out, emptying all the shells onto the floor. Fuck! I was stuck, and Chris sat at his desk like a statue. I knew the odds of them killing me were slim to none, but this whole extortion still had me on edge.

"My nigga, you need to hit that backside and get me some 100's, or imma start by killin' this lil' person you got workin' for you," he said and aimed his gun at Chris.

Chris tried hard to fight back his fear, but I knew on the inside he was shaking like a stripper. I huffed. Thunder had me pegged and could read me like a handbook. I spun around, and Calico followed me to the back, where I led them to my small wall safe. As I pressed the keypad, I spoke casually.

"I'm gon' bury you niggas for this shit. You gon' need this money to pay for your funeral."

He snickered at my words. "Says the man who got the gun to his head. You'll get your chance once a month; we'll be back, or my niggas gon' send fire in this bitch every day, ya feel me?" Calico said vehemently.

I sucked my teeth in. "You got what you came for, now beat it."

"Oh shit, one more thing before we go. Let yo lil' nigga know I got his aunty, and to send 10 bricks or that old bitch dead, ya feel me?"

He led me back into the lobby and then backed out of the building with Thunder. They all jumped into their cars and motorcaded out of the area, leaving Chris and I lookin' like bumps on a log.

I looked over to Chris. "Get your ass up."

This shit was about to get serious. Vrm, vrm, vrm. My phone buzzed. It was Nylon. We talked for a minute, and he dropped the bombshell on me about the money they owed Ackmed. I huffed and cursed a rant because I vouched for all this shit and knew it would make me just as liable as they were for it.

"A'ight, let me think of somethin'," I said before ending the call.

Zaro really needed to be out here right now. All this shit was bad. The Wolf Pack was two up on us now.

(ZARO)

DAYS LATER . . .

After I got the news about my aunt and the work being gone, I had a lot on my plate, especially being in jail. Nylon had got an extension on paying the ransom for my aunt, but that amount would be all I had to my name. If I came off all the work, with a few kilos left over that no one knew about, it was exactly enough to pay the ransom. I had paid Ackmed out of my own money that was leftover from the bank robbery and some of the coke that Kamar had given me. I was three kilos short from getting the job done still, though, so I had to make a plan. I decided to cut the shit so it was still potent, but would be enough to get my aunt back.

As I sat in my cell thinking of my next move, my phone buzzed in my hand—vrm, vrm, vrm. I glanced at the tag, and it was Ackmed.

"Fuck!" I muttered while thinking of something to say. I knew he was calling about the money.

Telay looked at me. "Who was that?" he asked, reading the expression on my face.

"Ackmed," I replied sharply.

"We got to get out of here," Telay shot back.

I nodded. He was right. I didn't bother to answer the call until I could talk to Nylon to see if they had some news I could use. My dad had sent Capo from Washington to help out, and they were supposed to be putting in work to help get my aunt back. For now, I needed to find another connect in order to get some money up to pay Saleen's people off before they came for us. This whole thing was spinning out of control.

While we talked about our next move, my name was called, so I stepped out the cell. Officer Wiggins stood at the gate waiting, so I said, "What's up?" as I strolled up to the gate.

"Your attorney's here," he answered and unlocked the bars.

I stepped out, fixing the collar on my jumpsuit, to see Frank sitting in the usual lawyer's den. He smiled as I entered. I already knew what was on his mind as I took a seat at the table.

"I suppose you're here for an answer to the note you wrote," I said.

"You can say that, but really I got some good news," he replied with a gingerly smile.

I shifted in my seat, ready for the good news. "What is it?" I asked anxiously.

"The feds dropped the bank robbery and the drug case on your crew."

I smiled as he spoke, but then came the however . . .

"However, the state police still got the murder charge pending on you. I can get that dropped easily if you can take care of that little thing with the Irish for me."

I curled my lip, then leaned back. "I can do that for you, but I need you to do something for me besides giving me my freedom."

Frank leaned in closer to hear me out. I knew he was interested because he wanted O'Mally out the way real bad. The question was: why did he want him out the way so bad? At the moment, it wasn't my concern. They deserved whatever they had coming anyway. They were all rats.

"What made the feds not want to indict on the bank case?" I asked curiously.

"You should have heard by now. They no longer have a credible snitch in the case."

I looked at him with raised brows. "What happened?" I asked curiously.

"O'Riley was stabbed numerous times by his roommate."

I did remember the jail going on lockdown a few days ago—the highlight of my day.

"I do, however, regret to tell you that your murder case is still on the table. Like I said, O'Mally is in the way, so if you can scratch my itch, I can rub yours," Frank said. He sounded like a guy from *The Sopranos* or one of them old mob movies. I even waited on him to say *capiche*. I chuckled lightly at his remark.

"You don't have to keep throwin' that shit with the Irish in the air. I'll handle that for you. Just get me out of this hellhole."

Frank leaned back in his seat with a smile. "Good, I'll get on that as soon as I leave here, and you'll make it in time for Kamar's party."

"Damn, that's fast," I said, and thought, if it were that easy, how come he couldn't have taken the retainer off? Why did I even have to kill for him to get out of jail? I kept these thoughts to myself.

"When would Telay and Bang be released?" I asked.

"Any moment. I faxed the paperwork before I came here," Frank replied, and just as he mentioned it, Wiggins showed up and motioned his hand in a circle, signaling for me to wrap things up. I drew my attention back to Frank, and we shook hands.

"That's good as done. Just make sure you get me out of here," I whispered to Frank.

C/O Wiggins led me back to my pod. Telay and Bang's paperwork had been completed as promised. Frank had done his part. Wiggins gave me the scoop on O'Riley as we walked, so I asked him about aiding with O'Mally.

"The best I can do for you is put you inside the pod. You'll have to figure the rest out on your own," he replied.

That was all I needed.

Before we hit the unit, he added, "I'll be back for your friends. Tell them to get ready."

I walked into the unit with Telay running up to me with a wide grin. "Bruh, we outta here!" he said excitedly.

"I already know. They keepin' me though, so I need you niggas to go out there and hold shit down for me. Frank says I'll be out soon though," I explained.

Telay dropped his head, his expression changing to one of somber. As we walked to the cell, Bang was getting his papers and pics together. I was kind of sick that we were being split up, but was happy for them nonetheless. Bang had asked me if I needed anything, and I told him the same thing—to hold shit down for me.

Fifteen minutes later, Wiggins was back to pick up Bang and Telay, and they left the unit in a rush, leaving Dog and me alone. I started to do my homework on O'Mally, and the more I found out about him, the harder it seemed it would be to kill him. Not the fact that he was one of those untouchable guys, but the fact that he was tough. Dog told me the dude used to be a UFC fighter, so it would be hard for me to get to him by myself.

I got an idea as I was talking to Dog though, and he noticed the expression on my face change.

"What you thinkin'?" he asked.

"What your case lookin' like?" I asked him.

"It's lookin' like I should get out soon, but I got a lot of hurdles to jump," he said.

"I might be able to get you out of here. I just need your help with some shit."

"I'm all ears," he said.

Then I gave him the rundown about the whole shit. I had to confirm the whole deal with Frank though, but I doubted it would be a problem. I dug my phone out to run it by him, as I would never divulge that kind of info over a jail phone. Frank was good with it. He just wanted us to take care of the situation.

I waited on Wiggins to do another round; I needed him to get Dog and me moved to O'Mally's unit. I'd have to secure a weapon for us to use, because from what I heard about O'Mally as a fighter, I was his size, so he'd probably have his way with me by himself. When them hyenas get on him though, it's gonna be a different story.

Wiggins came to the unit and agreed to get us moved to the other side of the jail tomorrow, so the only thing we had to worry about was the bikers—they might try to help him, so we'd have to get him quietly . . .

The next morning when Wiggins got on shift, he set it up for us to move to the unit. There was no turnin' back now. Dog and I went into our cell and started formulating our plan.

(TELAY)

Nylon and Zoo were parked in the Trackhawk, waiting for our release. It was time to get to work. Our to-do list was long. As we rode back to the projects, I felt a cold stare on my back, so I turned in my seat to find Zoo staring a hole in my back. This shit was crazy. I had no clue what this nigga had on his mind, but it was really starting to creep me out. He'd been doing this shit since before I went to jail, though, so I shook it off as if it were nothin'. I had to keep it to myself for now, I guess.

"Stop at the liquor store," Bang said.

"We got some liquor already at the crib, so be smooth," Nylon shot back. The lil' nigga had a different type of aura about him now. I looked around at the projects as we pulled up, and it felt like home sweet home. As we walked to the building, Nylon keyed the door open, and as soon as we walked in, everyone yelled, “Surprise!”

There was a house full of people, with a few add-ons to note. Nylon walked Bang and me around the party and introduced us to everyone. We came up on a little youngster that couldn't have been older than 14.

“This my lil' nigga Vern, he good with countin' money, and the lil' nigga a good shot,” he said with a smile, like a proud father.

“Was good, my baby,” I replied and shook his hand.

He stared at me as I did him the same. There was something familiar about the kid that I couldn’t put my finger on. He gave me a nod as a response, so I figured he just wasn’t much of a talker.

I looked back at Nylon and said, “We need to talk, we got some shit to handle,” while motioning for us to go someplace private. Nylon and I stepped into the kitchen and talked in hushed tones.

“Where y'all at with finding Zaro’s aunt and getting this money back? Saleen ain’t gonna take this shit lightly. We gone have to come up with some, or niggas gone be dead. Did you see how they did Flex?” I said.

Nylon didn’t respond, and I could tell he was tryin’ to conjure up something to say. He cleared his throat and said, “I’ve been doin’ this shit since you niggas been in jail. I got the situation under control. I got niggas out here lookin’ for her right now,” he replied defensively.

“Oh yeah? Look around, nigga. We at a fuckin’ surprise party when we got business to handle.”

“Boi, you need to chill. This ain’t that. You see all these shotters in here? This a meeting, dumbass nigga. I got all the people here. All the buildings been shut down so we can get these plans together, so don’t ever come at me like I’m slippin’,” he said methodically before putting his finger to my chest.

I didn't get to respond before Nylon added, "You're the one that needs to take a reality check. You the one that still got the case pending for being stupid. Boi, you gave the cops 100 G's. Niggas put a gun in Cowboy's face, had a shootout with us, and took the dope while you were layin' in a cell eatin' soups and shit, so miss me with that 'I'm home now' shit."

He looked me from head to toe and walked off. I was left speechless . . . I couldn't believe this nigga had just checked me in the rawest form. Just as I looked up, I felt that same cold stare on me. Zoo had overheard everything. He walked off, nodding his head, still mugging me. I was really about to check this nigga about all this shit, but I figured I would say something after our meeting; I wanted to catch him alone anyway. I ducked off into the bathroom for a minute to take the edge off and dug into my pocket for the packet of meth I'd scored from white boy Thomas right before Bang and I were released. I couldn't afford to tell Nylon to help me get some meth, as I'd been smoking it for a few months now, and it was how I stayed up for nights at a time with Willy Key. He smoked crack and never suspected me of anything because he'd never seen me get high. I contemplated how I would find more, knowing I would need it now that I'm putting in work. I knew I had to be careful though, with this nigga Zoo watching me like a hawk right now, so I called the only person I knew that would have some. Hopefully, his number hasn't changed.

Remo picked up on the second ring, "What's good, my boi? I heard you lil' niggas was freed," he said.

"Yeah, thanks, but fuck all that. I need to get in your face. You still got that motion?" I asked hungrily.

The line was silent while I awaited his response. I was anxious as all get-out.

"Yep, shit good, but I need some of that dog your boi neem got."

"I can make that happen. Text me what you want and I'll grab it."

"Where you at?"

"Projects, we can meet when I leave here. Give me about 20 minutes," I said and ended the call. I looked around, hoping that nosy-ass nigga Zoo wasn't lurking around, watching as he usually did. I had to break away for a moment to go and pick up the dope from my grandmother's house, as I still had half a key left over that no one knew about.

(REMO)

Shit was good while I was away from Flex. I had got mixed up with O'Mally and the bikers though because they had meth for a good price. I saw the opportunity and had to take it after jackin' Flex for the dope and money. I took it out of town and sold a lot to the bikers. They were lovin' it, so I had to get more, which is how I eventually linked up with Telay. Now I was back in business. I dialed up my people to let them know that I was about to meet up with Telay and told them it wouldn't take this dope fiend long to come runnin'.

"Hello, Curly, it's me. I'm about to meet up with Telay."

"Good, did you talk to him on the phone we gave you?" Curly Abotts said.

"No, but Imma call him back on it now. He called me."

"Okay, make sure you get him on the wire. Our new guy Keyonta and Shawnta will keep watch over you, so keep us posted."

I ended the call then went to my stash. Moments later, Telay's text came in, so I hit him back on the hot phone and got my shit together before leaving the house. I'd heard Thunder and Gambit were blowin' the city up and that they'd turned Rockford into a shooting range. I wouldn't be in the city for long, but I'd had business set up in South Dakota. My baby momma and I were teetering back and forth between the two places right now. I slid into my Benz truck and drove off slow. I popped in *Tekashi 6ix9ine*, he'd become my favorite rapper after taking my place with Curly Abotts.

I met Keyonta in the parking lot. He was noticeably younger than Abotts and Coats. Keyonta was black with a dreadhead kinda look, which definitely would help him go undetected in the hood. They had recruited him fresh out of the academy to do undercover work. He and Shawnta sat in the parking lot of the Denny's on Harrison and 11th St. It had started to rain as I looked around, making sure no one was watching, and pulled up next to them. I threw my hoodie over my head and hopped out my truck to slide into the back seat of their car. Shawnta was in the driver's seat and spun around to look at me.

"What you got for us today?" she asked.

"Telay wants to meet up, he's on his way to Levels," I said under the patter of windshield wipers moving side to side. The rain gave the interior of the car a secluded setting, almost as if the rain had hidden us from the rest of the world. I didn't have any worries on my mind at the moment.

"This could finally be our way into this new *Switch Gang Family*," Keyonta stated happily.

Shawnta went into the middle console and grabbed a small camera, which fit on my Gucci belt perfectly.

"We're gonna be able to hear and see everything with this. Before you get in the car, make sure you get us a view of his license plates" Shawnta said, passing me the device. Keyonta was excited to be on his first job, almost overly anxious to get to work.

I was ready too, but more just to get this thing over with. Once it was over, I planned to let them do their thing and jump on the highway back to the Dakotas with some heroin that they let me keep from the drugs they confiscated. I was playing Abotts and Coats to the maximum. I fitted myself with the camera, then slid into my Benz truck. I was headed to our meet spot when my phone chimed with a message. It was Telay, informing me that he was waiting on me at the Waffle House. I wasn't worried about Thunder or Calico intruding on our rendezvous because I had backup, Abotts and Coats watched over me. I found Telay around the back of the diner and pulled up beside him. I hopped out the Benz truck, making sure to catch his plates on the belt camera as I walked up to his car. I slid into the passenger seat and slapped hands with him.

"Is this that pure Afghan heroin?" I asked, noticing the baggie in the center console.

"Oh yeeha! This the batch Flex got killed over," he replied, chuckling. "Okay, this the aftermath from what I took from him. Ole stupid ass nigga," he said and laughed.

"It's cut with fentanyl, but still droppin' niggas, so you can put an easy 20 on it for sure," he said like any good salesman.

My eyes widened at the purity of the dope. It was a shame it had to go into an evidence locker. The way he spoke so freely about it and talked about the murder, I had to wonder what else he would talk about. I had this nigga dead to the wrong already, but I figured I'd just let him vent and see if I could get him to put Tiff's murder on Zaro. Now that would be a really big score for me.

"That's fucked up about Tif, why did Zaro murk the bitch?" I asked, knowing Shawnta was on the edge of her seat listening to the whole thing. Telay was fumbling with the bag of powder I'd given him. He took out a card full and crunched it down while I spoke on Tiffany's death. He stopped what he was doing and stared up at me. I thought maybe my cover was blown and looked down at the handle of his Glock in the car door. My heart began to thud rapidly.

Then a grin slid across his face. "That bitch killed herself for crossing the mob. She let that bitch-ass nigga Flex lead her to the other side."

He took a deep snort of the meth, then pinched the roof of his nose. “If she would’ve fucked with me, that bitch would be alive right now.”

I could tell he was feelin’ himself, as his eyes were glossy; this meth was as pure as water. I led him on to talk about all types of shit. The nigga was high out of his mind and even started talking about shit I hadn’t even asked about. This should be good enough for Shawnta to call Curly and make his fat ass go to the police evidence locker for me. After 20 minutes, I slid out the car. Telay had used me as a shoulder to lean on, and I had it all on audio. I hopped into my Benz and sped away.

(TELAY)

1 A.M.

I drove away from the Waffle House after meeting Remo to take the rest of the dope I had to the south side. I knew some bikers there that would buy the rest of it from me and put some extra money in my pocket. Right now, it seemed everybody was waging war, not getting money. Shit, I ain't even got no pussy since I'd been out of jail; don't get me wrong, Zaro was my nigga, but this ain’t what I signed up for. Bruiser’s people still ran the brothel/club while they were in jail, so I bee-lined there first. I was 5 minutes out when some bright lights flickered in my rearview mirror. I knew I could lose them in the Hellcat, so I tried my hand, hitting the gas pedal and—motor growling—before I knew it, I was doing 105. It felt like I was in a bullet as I cruised onto Harrison Road. There was no way they were gonna catch me. I listened to *Big Boogie Members Intro*, the lyrics and the meth had my adrenaline running. I pushed the cat to its limit, blowin’ through traffic with no regard for anyone's safety. I wasn't going back to jail—not on the same day I was released. I pulled out the bag of meth and snorted a huge pinch of it. The wheel swerved a bit, but I regained control.

The lights behind me seemed to have multiplied, they were coming at me from every angle, so I had to find another way. I went for the freeway where I could really open the motor up. I drove through Alpine recklessly as the rain continued to pour, obscuring my view somewhat. I didn't let that stop me, but as I came up on the exit, a car pulled out in front of me. I tried to brake and hydroplaned in a large puddle of water. I fishtailed as I moved the wheel from right to left, trying to regain control as the car spun out violently. I eventually went sideways, and as the car started to tip, I braced myself for impact. The Hellcat tumbled and flipped over while I was jolted around the car's cabin. It finally landed on its roof, and I must've blacked out, because when I woke up, the fire department was using the jaws of life to pry the doors off the car.

"This guy's lucky," the man said as they dragged me out.

"What's your name, fellow?" A female EMT asked while loading me into the ambulance.

"Te . . ." I said with a long pause. Suddenly, a female jumped in with us and cuffed me to the gurney; just like that, it was over.

"Fuck!" I muttered as the female cop smirked at me.

"Gotcha," she said, smiling.

(ZAMAD)

Lou and I talked on the phone for some time. He and I had done time together, and Kamar informed me Zaro needed a heroin connect to help get his aunt back. Lou was the man for fentanyl pills, he even had them cheap as Popeye's people. Because I had something different planned for them, I used Lou so there weren't any mob ties. I didn't want the dope tied to Zaro in any type of way, so I had to be sneaky on this mission. Lou could send 10 thousand fentanyl pills to cover what Zaro had to pay for the ransom, plus the money he owed Saleen. Kamar should've mentioned something to the Family about who Thunder really was. He's cold-hearted and doesn't love nothing. If Thunder felt they killed Flex, he was out to trade a life for a life. Even after he got paid the ransom, he was going to kill Sheila. He didn't value her life at all; she was just a victim of circumstances to him. Honestly, they were better off taking the money and getting a re-up than paying the ransom.

I sat in the cell making calls to help my son out, and after I finished setting it up for him to get the pills, I called Kamar to let him know that Lou was going to catch a flight out from LAX and was going to attend his party. I ended the call and sat back on my bed, staring out the window of my cell. U.S.P. Beaumont was a stressful place, and at times, the environment was ruthless; dudes had knives, and everybody was violent. Plus, there was always some shit goin' on, putting everyone on high alert. I stepped out the cell and took a stroll around the unit until the C/O shouted, "Mail call!" Everyone gathered around the office and listened for their name. I heard them call one of my guys and was geeked, as that meant the pack had landed. I hoped it wasn't copied as I went to my cell and waited.

30 minutes later, Jug-head and Trevor came in and both handed me a college booklet. I grabbed them greedily, examining the books. It was good, so I paid them both a brick of stamps worth 500 dollars and told them to pull back up on me. I flipped through the book, holding it up to the light . . . it was time to get money. I had just received 500 sheets of K2 worth at least 5 thousand a sheet. I had to drop some off on Popeye and his people before phase 2 of my plan could begin. Popeye and I had some unfinished business . . .

(VENTURE)

This was my third home since my brother had killed the G.D. I knew it wouldn't be the last. My mind drifted as I gazed out the window, my eyes parked on the basketball court. Memories of Calvin and Vernel plagued my thoughts. Most of my heart ached for my family back home. I was starting to miss the little things, like when Dad would make us pancakes on the weekend. He was always gone, but on Saturday mornings, he was there. A single tear streamed down my face as I thought about how life used to be for me. I was torn from my family by those men in bow-tied suits. I would one day find out who they were and make them pay. I didn't deserve this, but I didn't have any other family other than my Aunt Shawnta. Only if she knew I was here, I thought. Was she even notified?

I pondered back on the day of the funeral. I tried to recall if I'd seen her. Mrs. Whitmore stood in the doorway. She was a hag. My skin crawled at her sight. Her stares were creepy; however, Mr. Whitmore was the worst. "Dinner will be ready soon," she said. I glanced at her, not wanting to make eye contact.

"Okay, I'll be right down," I replied, then took a deep breath. All this was too much. I went to the restroom to get ready for dinner. I gazed into the mirror. The bags under my eyes were from the sleepless nights. I washed my hands, then cupped some water and rinsed my face. I could feel a pair of prying eyes sneaking over my back. I turned around, then jolted with fear. It was Mr. Whitmore standing in the doorway, looking like a hungry lion. He smiled.

"There's no need to be afraid," he said and shuffled off. He walked with a hunched-over back. His balding head and beady eyes made him look like a bald eagle. He stared at me with his water-blue eyes. I got the most eerie vibe. He backed out the doorway.

There were two other boys that lived at the house with us, and they were both scared and timid. Josh and I bumped into each other on my way downstairs.

"I see the way he looks at you. That's not good," he said out of nowhere, and continued on his path.

"What was that about?" I thought. He left me clueless.

"What are you talking about?" I asked as we both descended the steps, then cut in front of him. "Let me by."

"Not before you tell me what you're talking about first," he answered.

He scoffed. "Just stay out of Mr. Whitmore's line of sight," he replied and pushed past me. Josh was a nerdy, skinny little white kid. I followed him down for dinner. Timmy was the other boy in the house. His parents died in a car crash, from what I'd heard Mrs. Whitmore say on the phone. I hadn't said much to either of the boys. They were both quiet, from what I had gathered. This was the most Josh had said to me since I'd been at the house.

Mrs. Whitmore had made liver and asparagus. I looked at the plate of food, disgusted. The old man kept his sight trained on me, and she watched him. I was getting a very uncomfortable feeling.

"May I be excused, please?" I asked politely.

"You haven't touched any of your food," she answered with a smile.

"I'm not really hungry. I had a big lunch at school," I lied. My stomach rumbled with hunger pains. I couldn't bear to look at them any further. She nodded, and I walked away. I didn't know how much longer I could dodge Mr. Whitmore's sickly gaze. I darted upstairs to my room and cried. Moments later, Josh came up.

"He wants you. I can tell by the way he looks at you. You're not gonna be able to hide long."

Josh and I stayed up talking for a while. Timmy never came back.

The next morning, Timmy lay in bed sniffling. For Josh, this was all normal. I went to ask Timmy what happened, and he shooed me away. So Josh and I got ready for school as if nothing was wrong. I was curious as to what was going on. Timmy wouldn't speak to either of us. I noticed the scars on his back as he slid his shirt over his head. I had to try and get away from this house.

(SHAWNTA)

I sat at my cubicle, typing paperwork, when Abbotts walked in carrying a large file under his arm. Another guy followed him. I pegged the man for a fed with the Marshal Service.

"Attention, please, everyone," Abbotts said in a raised voice, getting everyone's attention in the office. We all looked up from our work. Keyonta spun around and perked up at attention.

He held the file high in the air as if it were a golden ticket. "This is a case file on SGF. The FBI is launching an investigation on them and wants us to take the lead since we're familiar with the suspects."

"So they're here to steal our work once again," I replied.

The guy behind Abbotts stepped forward and cleared his throat. "We've linked them to some terrorist cells that may be operating out of the city," he said while looking each of us in the eye, as if he were searching for a rebuttal. So I gave him one.

"How is that possible? These are local kids, born and raised in Rockford."

"And who are you to make such a determination?" he shot back.

"I apologize. My name is Randy Mitchell. I'm with Homeland Security. This is our link," he said, wheeling a packet with a tan, powdery substance.

"It's pure Afghanistan heroin that we can trace back to the Afghan mountains, outsourced by Al-Ad Darr," Mitchell explained.

"Ad Darr was number one on the FBI's most-wanted list years ago. I heard a team of army guys killed him in the mountains when I was at Quantico," I remarked.

"They did," this guy said.

“This guy Kamar is part of this drug ring somehow,” he continued.

“We got some intel that he is still here under the name of Saleen,” I stated.

“We also got the group under investigation for the murder of Kimberly Yantze, the city’s D.A.,” Abbotts tagged in. He narrowed his eyes in my direction. Abbotts knew Kim and I were siblings. As the agent continued talking on the case, I drifted off. I hated how Kim spent her leisure time. Her marriage to a drug dealer put a major strain on our relationship.

Abbotts took a seat next to me, and I knew what was coming next.

“Save it,” I sighed.

“Your sister was a good D.A. Her boys deserve more than what they’re getting,” he said.

His comment had struck a nerve. “Yes, but I just hate the fact that she slept with and had children with that drug dealer,” I said, shaking my head.

“You’re the only family they have,” Abbotts stated. “I wanted to inform you that the youngest boy, Calvin, is in juvie for murder, while the other, Vernell, is a runaway. Venture is being held at the Whitmore house.”

That name had some familiarity to it, and I searched my memory for any recollection, ultimately writing it off for the time being. I promised Abbotts I would do something about Calvin’s situation, and he grunted before wiggling his way out of the chair. Keyonta looked at me with a smirk on his face.

“So this means we’re part of the FBI!” he exclaimed, while I scoffed, going back to work.

(KAMAR)

I sat across from Frank. His office was a very pricey place; I admired it, even wanting to have my own place this plush. He gave me the updates on Zaro's case.

"It is detrimental that Zaro attends this party," I said.

He nodded and leaned back in his chair. "Just give me a little time and I'll make something happen," he answered.

"How soon do you think? This party is a big thing, and I'm turning everything over to him. It's a meet and greet; it's time for me to hang up my hat for good," I said, lighting a 200-dollar cigar.

Frank looked at me in disbelief, so I switched topics and asked about Zamad. "The Supreme Court shot his appeal down months ago."

I frowned because what he'd told me contradicted what Zamad was saying. "Are you sure about that?" I asked.

"I'm positive."

"That's odd because he's talking like he's about to get out soon."

"I can look into it for you if you'd like, but his business with me and the courts has been finalized. It would take an act of Congress or an escape to get him out now."

I was baffled by what I was hearing but wasn't sure if I should divulge any further. After thinking on it though, I figured if he wanted me to know, he would have told me, so I just shook my head.

"Just be on standby if we need you. For now, let's focus on this thing with Thunder right now," I remarked as his eyes widened at the mention of his name.

"How the hell did he get out? I thought he was serving life in the state—him and that cousin of yours, Gambit," he said.

"Yeah, me too. I've been beating myself up trying to figure it out myself," I replied.

"Ok, I'll take a look at it."

I rose from my seat to leave and pulled out a large envelope, dropping it on the desk. Frank was mob-tied. He wasn't your ordinary lawyer, but he was connected in all the important circles.

“Maybe this will make you work a little faster,” I remarked, shoving the money-filled envelope at him.

“My kind of guy,” he said with a sly grin.

I hit the auto start on my Ferrari and slid into the front seat. I tapped the gas pedal and fishtailed out of the parking lot. Finesse2tymes blared through the speakers. I drove down Forest Hills feeling the vibe. I was playing Thunder like a game of chess. I had to make some sacrifices; I needed Zaro out of jail for this to work. Once this party commenced, things would come together.

“Chess, not checkers,” I muttered as I pulled up at the Coliseum. I was met by the planners. The men were loading all the sound equipment into the club. I booked the hottest artists to show up. I had OTA booked to run security. Moneybagg Yo, Lil Durk, Lil Jay, Bam, and Shakespeare were going to perform on stage. OTA was standing on business in the industry. They all represented Saleen. He was all for the betterment of the Acks. Saleen was their Imam.

I anticipated Thunder would try to crash the party. This would be where his career would end. ATM was on standby. I wanted to put Zaro in position with them. I sat in my Ferrari, watching the men work. A black F-150 pulled up on me fast with tinted windows. I was quick on the draw with my Glock 23. Two twin boys popped up from the bed like jack-in-the-boxes. I thought my vision was crossed, seeing the twins.

“Slow down, OG,” one of them said. Then the window came down. Calico was the driver, and Thunder looked over at me with bloodshot eyes.

“Yooo,” he said in a raspy voice from the cup he was sipping on. “Calm down, soldier. I'm just checking you out,” he said with his sight set on my new Ferrari. I smirked, then chuckled, knowing what was about to come. I just hoped it wouldn't.

"Niggas got new whips out here, and I ain't get one," he said slyly. This was him on his bullshit, I thought. Calico snickered.

"What you want right now, Thunder? I see you out here on demon time. How much?" I asked, frustrated.

He smirked and rolled his head around. "How much you pay for the Rarri?"

I shook my head. Then one of the little ones jumped out the bed of the truck. Shorty slid in my shit like a snake and skirted off. I went for my glizzy. I contemplated putting his brains on the windshield as he sped off. Thunder had me frozen with his weapon out, guarding his shorty's antics. There was no way out. I had to use my head on this one. It took everything in me not to fill the back window with holes as he sped up the road.

"You don't buy shit without my say. I'm the IRS. I get half of whatever you get. Sell a nickel rock, I want 2.50, ya dig!" He mugged me, then Tee Grizzly played loudly as they pulled off, leaving me looking like Joe Sausage Head.

I pulled out my iPhone to call a ride. Chris picked up on the first ring. I instructed him to bring me something low-key to drive in. I dialed Nylon. I needed some security until I could figure something out with Thunder. The cake was in the oven on him. After my party, I planned on sending the ATM. I had to position my pieces in the right place.

Chris pulled up, and I plopped in the front seat. I was on fire.

"Where's the Ferrari?" he asked. Here we go with a thousand questions.

I laid my head back and went into deep thought.

Chapter 7

(ZOO)

I drove behind the smoke tint of my Ram truck. My F/N laid across my lap as I followed Telay down West State Street. He didn't know I was tailing him. Lately, he'd been acting funny since the high-speed chase that put him in the hospital a few nights ago. He'd been moving strangely ever since. He was already acting wired, but now he was sneaking around. He and Zaro grew up together, but that shit didn't mean nothing to me. I wasn't going down for nobody.

Telay turned into the Waffle House parking lot. I watched as he slid next to an Impala with tint. I couldn't get a good look at the occupants, but there was a female driving. He looked around nervously as he slid into the back seat. I parked in the cut and watched from afar. Twenty minutes passed, and he slid out of the back seat. That was odd, I thought. I continued to tail him. He ended up going to his grandmother's house, then back to the projects. I wondered who he talked to in the Impala. I sat in my truck outside the front building in Concord. Cowboy pulled up in his Hellcat and parked next to me. The window came down.

"Nylon out here?" he asked.

I shrugged. "I don't know. I just pulled up, fam. We need to talk though," I replied.

He scrunched his face up. "What's the business?"

"It's about ya man Telay. Nigga acting funny out here, like he feds or some."

He laughed. “You tweaking. Telay hate the police. I can't let you put that on my nigga with no proof.”

“Telay good, fam. I think you paranoid right now. The nigga just got out. Frank don’t fuck with rats, my baby,” he stated firmly.

I dropped my head. I didn’t know what to say from that point. Telay was their best friend. I brought it to Zaro when he was out, and his response was the same. Maybe I was tweaking, I thought. I was still curious as to who he was talking to in that Impala.

“If you see Nylon, let him know I’m out here. I’m going to check on Rene,” Cowboy said, then pulled off.

Telay was sitting on the couch playing the PS5 when I walked in. He was into a deep game of Madden. I sat next to him as he and R1 jerked the controllers.

“What does R1 stand for?” I asked.

He chuckled. “Are you serious?” he said, staring up at me curiously.

“Real shit.”

“It’s the trigger button on the Xbox. Duh.”

I shrugged my shoulders; it made sense. Telay jumped with excitement that he'd won the game. R1 blamed his defeat on me for making the distraction. Capo walked in amped up.

“Look at this,” he said, holding his iPhone in his palm. He brought up a video on Instagram. I watched the video in disbelief. I jumped out of my seat, heated.

“This shit really getting out of pocket!” I exclaimed.

“What is it?” Telay asked.

I passed the phone off to him. “We got to do something about this,” Telay replied. We watched Kamar get his Ferrari taken. The caption read: Spanking All You Rockford Niggas. This meant they had waged war on everybody in the city.

“What now, gang?” Capo asked.

Vrm, vrm, vrm. My phone buzzed. It was Nylon.

“Yoo!” I answered. It sounded like he was out of breath—something was definitely off.

“Fam, I need you and Telay to get over here,” he said frantically, then ended the call abruptly. I looked at the phone like it was deadly. “Over where?” I thought to myself as I held the phone with a skeptical glare. Telay noticed the look on my face.

“Who was that?” he asked.

“It was Nylon. He wants us to meet him, but I don’t know where he called from.” I tried to call him back, but it rang to voicemail. I tried it again and got the same result. Telay stood up, clearly upset.

“Dammit!” he said and punched the air.

“What now?” Capo said, awaiting orders.

I tried to hit Nylon's line one more time, but still got no answer. The shit was stressful. We all stepped out of the building in sync. Cowboy was talking to Crystal on her car window. I pulled him to the side and informed him what was going on. He immediately was ready to find something out.

(ZARO)

I stalked O’Mally as if he were shark food. O’Mally strutted the pod as if he were the apex predator. Dog and I, everyone feared him, but we viewed him as our meal. We had two nice blades to put in him, made out of the bunk. It took two days to carve them out. We stayed to ourselves on the unit in order not to draw any attention. I sat and watched Monday night football while keeping my line of sight on him. Dog was looking at his tablet. I looked over at Dog and signaled for him to meet me in the cell. Moments later, we both talked about our next move. It was becoming harder to get at O’Mally, and our time was dwindling down.

“This shit don't look good right now,” Dog said.

“I got an idea. Ima holla at Wiggins and see if he'll assist. We got to hurry up and get the job done. Kamar's party is in less than a week. I'm not trying to be stuck in jail for that," I replied.

Two hours later, I got C/O Wiggins to pull me into the hallway, and we came up with a plan to get O'Mally away from everyone else. The next day came about. Wiggins had said he'd be able to shut the cameras down for at least five minutes. He would put me on the laundry detail. O'Mally worked the halls at night; it would be the perfect time. He would disguise it as a deal gone bad or some random bullshit. The cameras would be down for five minutes or so. We had to work quickly; it would only work if we got him by surprise.

3:30 AM, Wiggins came to the unit to let us out. O'Mally stood tall. He put his shirt on, and I noticed how muscular he was. It was almost intimidating, but that's why Dog and I both had what they called "bone crushers." I was ready to carve him like a turkey. We all lined the hallway wall. Dog rubbed his eyes. I could tell he'd just woken up. He didn't look as if he were bothered by anything. I guess I had too much stress on my mind because I was wired up. My aunt Sheila had been kidnapped, and we still owed the connect a half a mil. Shit was all bad, but this could put me back in the game if I could get away smooth with killing O'Mally.

"Form a single file line," the guard asked. Everyone did as they were told. Once we got to the corridor, we split and went to our respective job assignments. I walked behind O'Mally. I was overly anxious to get the job done. The metal blade was concealed in my shoe. I had to get it out soon. Once we got to the laundry room, the sounds of the machines would muffle any other sounds that might emit from the room. This was the perfect kill zone.

Dog and I were met by another black guy.

"What's good, ackees? My name is Aziz," he said, holding his hand out for us to shake.

Dog and I both stared at each other with confusion. Our understanding was that we would be alone with O'Mally.

Now it seemed like the hit was slipping away from us. It was presenting a major challenge.

“What's up, ackees? Y'all the new help? I'm Aziz,” he gave his introduction. Beep! Beep! His watch beeped. He checked the time.

“I got to make wudu, y'all hold tight, I got to make salat,” he said.

“I'm...” Before I could get my name out, he stopped me.

“I know who you are. I'll run it with you when I'm done praying,” he said, then walked off. The whole scene was baffling, but this was the only chance we had.

“What now?” Dog asked, looking around.

“We continue on as expected,” I said, then went into my shoe. I slid the 8-inch blade from beneath the sole. Dog followed my lead. O’Mally was in the back pushing a large bin of clothes. The laundry department was large; it afforded us enough room to keep the hit discreet. Aziz was on the other end of the room behind a half wall on his knees praying. This was our time to go and handle the business. Wiggins walked by and gave us a head nod—that was the cue, letting us know that the cameras were down.

“Let's go,” I said to Dog. He was on go mode, ready. O’Mally was busy with a load of clothes at the dryer when I walked up. He spun around. He'd seen us using his sixth sense.

“Young laity, want to try the luck of the Irish?” he spat in a heavy Boston accent. O’Mally had a sick sense for welcoming imminent force. He smiled at the threat of death. He readied himself for war, cracked his knuckles, and popped his neck. I slid the large knife from my sleeve like Wolverine releasing his claws. His eyes bulged as he gawked at the metal gripped in my palm. Dog stood erect with his metal out. We were bloodthirsty.

“Let’s work,” he said, then tried to take a swing at me. I stumbled backward. Dog ran up on him, swinging his knife. He sliced his arm. “Aha,” he grunted.

I regained my composure. The punch felt like I'd been hit by a baseball bat. O'Mally motioned toward Dog swiftly. I darted at him with the point of my knife leading the way. I punctured his back. I could feel his flesh rip open. He fell forward and gripped Dog, shoving him to the wall, unfazed. I stabbed him a second time. The sound of his bone crunching made me cringe.

"Ahhh!!" he wailed and winced with pain.

I thought he would go down, but he turned back around and faced me. This guy was like the Terminator. Dog and I were on him like a pack of hyenas on a ferocious lion. We stabbed him repeatedly. His blood saturated my jumpsuit. He finally collapsed after a three-minute struggle. My chest heaved. Dog laid on the ground clutching his side.

"That big-ass cracker knocked the wind out of me," he said, gripping his side. I, too, was in agonizing pain, rubbing my arm. I walked over to help Dog up.

"You good?" I asked, looking at his wound. I helped him to his feet.

"We got to get out of here," he said, stealing a glance at O'Mally.

I walked over to him and kneeled down, hovering over his body. He fought for air. I planted my blade in his chest. As I looked him in the eye, I twisted the knife. "Frank sends his regards," I said, and he spit a glob of blood in my face before the reaper came for his soul.

Aziz walked in. He looked at me, then at O'Mally.

"Damn, what happened, ack?" he asked with concern. I froze up, knowing we were caught. I couldn't go out like this. My first thought was to get Aziz, but neither Dog nor I had the energy to fight anymore. My chest heaved up and down.

"Fear not, ackee. I'm no snitch. I got you a change out of those clothes, and I can bandage y'all up," he said sincerely. I had heard about Sunni Muslims. I had no other choice but to trust him. I hoped this wouldn't come back to bite me. I allowed Aziz to help us.

"This way, ack. Wiggins will be back through soon. How do you think I knew who you were? I'm here to help."

I was somewhat relieved to hear that.

"How do you know Wiggins?" I asked, as he walked us over to a storage room. He pulled out a change of clothes and bandages like he'd expected this to happen.

"Everything is good, Ack. I'm OTA. Kamar sent me to back y'all up. He's posting my bond tomorrow. I'm your backup plan."

I smiled. Kamar was on point with everything. Aziz went and snapped the pics of O'Mally's dead body for his confirmation. We dumped O'Mally's body where it couldn't be found for a while.

"Ack, if you don't mind, what does OTA mean?"

He snickered. "Only the Muslims."

(FRANK)

5 A.M.

My phone pinged with a message. I rolled over and glanced at the time—it was 5 a.m. "Time for me to get ready for work," I muttered, grabbing my phone. I checked the message, and a sick grin spread across my face as I stared at O'Mally's lifeless body. Finally, that nigga was gone for good. All that shit was behind me now.

I bounced to my closet, ready to uphold my end of the deal for Zaro and his boy. I dug out a few photos, looked at them with a devilish grin, then shoved them into Zaro's file. I threw on a fresh Michael Kors suit, snapped the Audemars onto my wrist, adjusted my cufflinks, and fixed my collar as I stared at myself in the mirror.

I rode the elevator down to the front lobby of the Trump Tower in downtown Chicago. My office was out of Rockford. By 8 a.m. I had to be at court for Zaro at 9 a.m. I was confident I could get him off. Rockford was an hour out. As I hit the Dan Ryan, I ran into heavy traffic

(ZARO)

I sat in the bullpen, waiting on the bailiff to come in. I was starting to pace; the bullpen was small and crowded. I shook my head and cursed under my breath. Everyone sat with their heads low, saying silent prayers, hoping they'd get out of jail. I knew I was guilty and had no chance of beating my case. Frank was the only prayer I silently hoped for. I just hoped they didn't notice O'Mally was MIA until I was done with court. Wiggins would keep the body out of sight.

"Mr. . . . Monson?" My last name was called over the inmate chatter at the front gate. I jumped to attention and snaked my way through the men. I looked to see Frank, but instead, it was a public defender.

"Are you Mr. Monson?" a fine, light-skinned young lady asked. She introduced herself as Ms. Summers. I admired her beauty.

"Yes, that's me."

"Your lawyer hasn't showed up yet and the judge is about to call you. The state has a plea ready for you today," Ms. Summers said. I looked at her like she had something in her teeth.

"Your attorney's not here today. We're supposed to go to trial, so I have to notify you of any offer."

I figured I'd stall long enough for Frank to arrive. "Okay, what is it?" I asked.

"Five years. You'll serve two years, six months of that," she said proudly. I scoffed.

"For murder, nigga? I'll run with that. Let me get that same plea," one of the men in the bullpen remarked. All of a sudden, everyone had something to say. The offer was good, but if they only knew what I'd been through. Truth be told, I wanted to take it on the strength. I was lookin' at life and a minimum of thirty years. Time was ticking.

"I need a response," she said in a soft but demanding tone. It was kind of sexy in a way.

I thought hard about it and realized my plans were about to crumble. I agreed to the plea. The woman pushed the papers into the bars. I signed them, and she ushered me back to the courtroom. Moments after, I was summoned in. I walked down the hallway, ball and chain . . .

(COWBOY)

Telay walked into the small apartment, huffing in frustration as he sat the duffle bag on the table in front of me. I gawked at it suspiciously, figuring there was something about it he didn't agree with.

"What is that?" I asked, nodding at the bag.

"190 thousand. We short 10 bandz," he replied.

I shook my head. The deadline for Sheila was in less than two hours. Thunder had already given us an ample amount of extensions.

"Them niggas should be good with what we got. This is more than enough money," Telay stated, staring at the bricks of money. I twisted my lip and shook my head uncertain. I honestly thought the worst for Sheila. It appeared they were going to kill her either way. I wasn't sure if I was the only person that could see that or not. The deadline had been extended too many times. We had to come up with a contingency plan to get Ackmed his money and keep a flow going in the PJs.

"Has anybody heard from Nylon?" I asked. This was Nylon's job.

"Try calling him again," I said.

Telay pulled his phone out to try Nylon—no avail. There was nothing.

Vrm, vrm, vrm. My phone buzzed. It was Crystal. I'd almost forgotten we had a date set for tonight. It was our three-month anniversary. Unfortunately, I had to reschedule. I had to take over for Nylon.

The door opened, and Vernal walked into the room. We all looked at him.

"Where's Nylon?" I asked.

He shrugged and handed me a knot of twenties.

"What's this?" I asked.

"A band from the morning shift."

I looked at the money as if it could have been more. I noticed he'd been putting in a lot of work since Nylon took him on. He had been working the spot 24 hours—he practically lived here.

"This it?"

"Yeah, shit was slow."

I drew my attention to Capo and let him know I was going to need him to make the drop to get Sheila back. He asked about the money being short. My first mind wanted to tell him to light the block up. R1 and R2 looked like hyenas—these lil niggas were there for that purpose. Capo must have read my thoughts. He gave me a serious stare.

"What's the use of having shooters if you ain't gone use 'em, cuz?"

I knew exactly what he meant. I peered down at all the switches and drums. I had to make the right call. Sheila's life was partially in my hands. Before I could speak, Capo stepped away to answer his phone. When he stepped back into the room, he had a wide grin on his face. I looked at him with a glimmer of hope.

"That was Zamad. He got that connect for us. We need to get up to Indiana. His people got 10 thousand fentanyl pills waiting on me to pull up."

I took a deep breath, half relieved. However, I still had to make the call about how to handle the drop.

"What's the deal on the ole lady, cuz?" he asked.

"They gon' kill her anyway. So when y'all get there, if it look funny, waste no time and air that bitch out. Ya feel me?" I said. I thought against it, but the way I could see it, Auntie was good as dead either way. They just wanted the money—it was just a consolation prize.

Chapter 8

(NYLON)

"Where is my money? You've had the product for weeks now, and I've been calling, no return on my calls or nothing," Ack said angrily.

"You ain't have to do all this. We're gonna get your money," I replied confidently. Being held captive in the basement of their masjid, I had to keep a positive mind. The men patrolled with AKs. I looked around for a way out, but there was nothing.

"I think your people need to know I'm serious about my money. You've been dragging me along like a rag doll," Ack said, his demeanor calm, but menacing. There was a cold vibe in the air.

"We got the money, shit just ain't going as it should right now."

Ackmed had a forever resting serious face. He had a thick beard, and his eyes were dark. Ack's background was mysterious.

"Who do you want to call that will want to pay for your safety?" Ack asked heartlessly.

I dropped my head shamefully. I had let Zaro down. He'd left me in charge, and now we had no connect because of me. Zaro was the only person I knew that would help.

"We should kill the American. They have no morals. I warned Saleen of this. He puts too much trust in them," Jihad remarked.

I knew Ackmed worked for Saleen, but I was curious who Jihad was. His character said stone-cold killer, and his actions said he was appalled by anyone who wasn't Muslim. Ack-Med had some empathy for the non-Muslims. These OTA dudes lived by pride, honesty, and trust. Most of all, they hated to be lied to. My life was dependent on my honesty, and I was showing no code of honor. OTA was becoming a name from Rockford to Chicago. This was something they were accustomed to in their country.

Jihad circled me methodically. My heart drummed from fear. There was a possibility that I could die right here and now. He pulled a dagger from the side pocket of his Afghan army pants. His eyes had death behind them. I had to accept my fate. The air had suddenly saturated with murder vibes. *Damn*, I thought. Zaro was supposed to be home right now, and I was about to die.

"I'll give you one chance to call someone and see if they value your life. Saleen is more sympathetic than I. He says to give you another chance; however, your distrust is what's on trial here, the money isn't," he spoke with venom. His words pierced me like needles. I watched his every move, praying he wouldn't spaz out. Jihad passed him an iPhone.

"Whom shall I call? I'll give them one chance to save your life or this will be the end for you."

I took a deep breath. I looked around at the men. I had a huge choice to make. I thought about whose number I should give him. I wondered if Zaro made it home this morning. I didn't want to waste my call.

"Fuck," I muttered.

Jihad looked at me impatiently.

(COWBOY)

I was sure Zaro would've reached out by now to one of us— we all needed him right now. This was all his mess that we were in, and Thunder came for us hard. I looked at the caller ID on my phone as it buzzed in my lap. I really didn't feel like talking right now; I had to stay focused on this new connect we were about to meet. None of us even knew these guys or anything about them. Capo said he and Zamad dealt with them while they were in prison. He mentioned they had connections to a black hand down at USP Beaumont. He talked about them highly. The good thing about the trip was I didn't have to risk no money. We were working out some courtesy of Zamad.

Capo exited the highway. My phone continued to buzz. I turned the screen toward Capo. "You recognize this number?" I asked. He shook his head no. I finally answered.

"What?" I said, annoyed that they'd let the phone ring this long instead of getting to the point, and ended the call.

"That's no way to speak to a dear friend," the man said in a foreign accent.

"Who is this?" I asked, curiously trying to catch the voice. I thought it might've been a prank call.

"I got your friend here, and we're looking to have a moment of clarity," the caller spoke calmly.

I frowned, my face wondering who was on the other end of this phone playing with me. I was almost about to end the call. I was way too stressed to play some childish games. "Humor me. Who is this, and what do you want?" I replied.

He laughed menacingly. Somehow, I knew he meant business. "I am the archangel of death, and I want my money. Your friend would like to negotiate with his life for your version of the truth," the caller said.

I scrunched my face angrily, then Nylon got on the phone. I shifted in my seat. "Nylon, where you at?" I asked anxiously.

(KAMAR)

I walked over to my mini bar in the privacy of my condo. I tipped a bottle of Remy 1738 straight up, *Finesse2tymes* filled the airwaves. I replayed the day's events of the lil' goons jacking my car. All I could think about was murder. Gambit was my cousin. I knew I would have to kill him too. There was no love in the heart of the city. Gambit hadn't personally done anything, but he was guilty by association. My vengeance was coming soon. I swallowed the liquor hard and frowned.

Two Glock 19s, two FNs, and three MAC-90s decorated my glass tabletop. The only reason I hadn't taken Thunder on straight up was I had too much at stake. Zaro was supposed to take over. I had no time to play childish games with him. I wanted OTA to link with us. I owed Zaro that much. I wasn't sure if I could keep my demon at bay much longer.

I picked up my Glock 19. I held it upright, my eyes scanned its craftsmanship. I felt my dick harden at the thought of putting a bullet in Thunder's head.

"Not now, this shit is chess, not checkers," I muttered, reminding myself what I had to do. I rolled a blunt of some exotic to ease the tension in my mind. I took another swig of the bottle. The liquor started to play on me. I picked up the phone and called Gambit. He answered on the first ring.

"What's up, cuz?" I said, in a friendly tone.

He chuckled at my sarcasm. "What you want, fam? This ain't like you."

"I need to talk to you about ya man," I said.

"Who?"

"Calico and Thunder."

"Ha, ha, ha," he laughed. "A'ight, you sure this what you want?"

"Why wouldn't I? We still family, ain't we? Let's have some drinks at the bar on me," I said.

The line was silent for a minute. Then he replied, "Come and get me. I'm at Isha's house."

I left my condo hoping I could solve this thing with Thunder through Gambit. Blood was thicker than mud, is what I told myself as I slid into my Hellcat. I rolled the window down as I pulled out the parking garage. The night's air was crisp. I could smell death in the air. It loomed all around. I was oblivious to where.

I drove to Gambit's baby mama's house. She stayed on the South Side near the Lucky 7 bar. I called him when I got close. He stepped out the house. Gambit hadn't been out of jail two weeks, and he already had his hands in some of everything.

My plan was to get him drunk and see what type of handle I could get on Thunder. Gambit stepped out the house, looking around in the darkness. He clutched his gun as he approached my car. He slid into the passenger seat and laid the gun on his lap. I looked down at it and smirked.

"Did you really need to bring that?" I said jokingly, but I respected the code of the streets.

"Better to have it than die without it. You might be trying to up the score."

I chuckled and stared at him with disappointment. I knew he was being sarcastic about the whole thing. However, there was some hint of how he really felt. "Why would you say that? Blood is thicker than mud, right?" I waited for his response.

I turned into Stash O'Neal's Sports Bar. We had to leave our pipes in the car. Once we were in the bar, we finished our conversation while taking shots. The more we talked, I felt like he was driven to defend Thunder at any cost. He was hell-bent on me killing Flex. So I changed my tactic.

"Ya man's keepin' shit goin' with this extortion shit he put on me. It's starting to get old."

Gambit cut his eye at me. He studied my candor, then shook his head in dismay.

"Thunder like a brother to me. You and I are just cousins, distant at that. You drew first blood by having them Arabs kill Flex."

"You don't know that. It's only an assumption," I replied. Where were they getting their information from? I thought as Gambit and I both, in sync, knocked back a double shot of Patron and slammed the glass on the table.

"Wooo! Keep 'em coming," Gambit shouted at the sexy lil' thang that served us. She looked back at him with a smile and sashayed away. Her round ass had us both in a trance, almost making me forget my objective. I shook the sexual thoughts I had for her, then went back to Gambit.

"Can you tell Thunder to ease up on me?"

He laughed. "Nigga, you started this, not me."

I smiled at him, frustrated by his stubbornness. I held my drink up and downed it. "My nigga," I said, lighting a $200 cigar.

Our drinks kept coming. By the end of the night, we were both wasted. We'd drunk two fifths of Patron and a bottle of Spade. I was lit, goin' to my car, so was Gambit. We agreed to spend the night at my condo. We left the bar around 3 a.m. I barely made it to my condo. We both stumbled inside. I walked over to the mini bar.

Chapter 9

(ZAMAD)

2008

My Cutlass Supreme rested on 24-inch blades that gleamed in the sun. I was the center of attention in my projects. Kamar had his seat all the way back, a 9 milli lay across his lap. Flex, Thunder, Gambit, Calico, Kamar, and myself had the projects on lock. Concord Commons was our building. We were jack boys, but we kept our people fed.

"I rolled my head in Kamar's direction. You gonna fight that white man's war?" I said, looking at Kamar. I fumed over his departure for the army. Kamar and I had been the best of friends as long as anybody could remember.

"You act like I'm 'bout to go get killed. Maybe I'll come back with a plug or something. You know them Arabs got all the heroin," he said.

Kamar was an opportunist. He always had something in play. As we talked, Flex and Thunder slid up. They hopped out, looking hungry. Thunder gazed at the rims on my ride and complemented me. My niggas were straight wolves.

"I see who out here getting the money," he said.

"Stop it," I replied with a smile.

"What's up with that move you had?" he asked, in a more serious tone.

I hopped out the car and met him at the hood. We all slapped hands, greeting each other, ready to get to work. Gambit rolled up with Calico in unison. Once we were all present, I put them up on the plan like Thunder had asked me about.

"It's gonna be close to a mill in it for us," I said.

Everyone looked at each other with disbelief. This was the most we'd ever hit for. It would take us out the ghetto for good.

"Speak on it," Flex said, anxiously, while rubbing his hands together like a fly over food. I started by telling them about Popeye, a cartel member who shipped the dope.

"They good for at least thirty keys. We gonna have to stay masked up and go in with murder vibes. Them Mexicans will die for that coke," I stated.

"Muthafucka good as dead in my book. Ya dig?" Thunder remarked.

I continued to go over my plan methodically. After I finished, my niggas were all in and ready to press play.

TWO DAYS LATER . . .

The small house was sectioned off by a short wooden picket fence. However, as the Spanish guy walked the perimeter of the house, I knew he had to be armed.

"This gon' be like takin' candy from a baby. I think dude strapped," I said, pointing in the man's direction with ease, while keeping my sight on the house like a venomous snake watching its prey.

"Baby better be good or I'ma spank that ass," Thunder said.

I laughed at him and clutched my Millennium, stayin' focused as I watched an Escalade pull up in the driveway. A younger kid draped in gold hopped out, clutching a duffle bag. I perked up in my seat, knowing this was it. Our eyes were trained on the target before us.

We dressed as cops to catch them off guard. It was noted that the occupants of the home were English-deficient, but I was sure they'd understand badges when we breached the door. I held the Nextel chirp to my mouth, then hit everyone involved. Ber! Ber! My chirp bleeped. “Everybody ready?” I asked, holding the mic to my mouth.

Everyone hit back, “It's a go.”

We bolted from the cars. Kamar carried the battering ram. I counted to three, and he crashed the door with great force. It took one swing. BOOM! The door flew off the hinges like a leaf blowing in the wind. Our entry was tactical, making it seem that much real. Flex threw a flashbang inside—BOW! The flash temporarily blinded them, then Thunder, Calico, and I rushed in, guns out. The Mexicans scattered about the house like migrating ants as we breached the foyer.

“*Boca! Boca!*” I spun to the sight of Thunder firing off rounds into the ceiling. I shot him a dissatisfying glance—it wasn’t part of the plan. However, it worked in our favor. All the movement ceased.

“Policía! Everybody on the floor!!!” I shouted in Spanish, keeping to the police routine as they hit the floor. The men began to speak; they pleaded not to go to immigration. They thought we were ICE agents.

Calico zip-tied the occupants of the house and lined them all up against the wall in the living room. I strolled down the line, looking for the guy who pulled up in the Cadillac truck. I found him with his head down, trying to hide. He knew I wanted him. I snatched him up by the collar.

“Where that bag at?” I hissed in his face.

“No hablo inglés,” he said, tryin' to trick me with the no-English routine. But it didn't work; I was fluent in Spanish. Thunder slid his mask off. I cut my eye at him—I sensed he was 'bout to do something stupid. I spoke in Spanish to the courier, demanding he tell me where the dope was. As I expected, he declined to tell me. I tried to reason with them and assure them we weren’t ICE and they could pay us off to avoid jail. Hopefully, they'd offer up the stash. They talked it over.

The house supervisor took charge, and he spoke quickly. He was resistant to give up the dope, but the others pleaded with him to save their lives. They all feared being deported more than anything—the dope had no bearing on their decision-making. I confirmed to them we weren't ICE agents. The man turned his head, letting me know he was done talking.

"It's in the back room," Goldy mumbled, throwing me off guard.

"Fuck he say?" Thunder snapped.

I moved closer, told him to repeat it, and he did. Suddenly, the men started speaking in Spanish rapidly. They went back and forth with each other. The leader had told him that Popeye would murder their families—the cartels had a strong hold over them. He turned toward me and, in English, spoke, "It's in the wall. Just don't kill us," the man pleaded.

Thunder didn't waste any time. He darted out of the room. Moments later, I heard a loud thud. Calico and I kept our guns on the hostages, making sure they didn't try anything stupid. Flex returned with two duffle bags and dropped them on the floor. Thunder dragged a large trunk with a lock on it. I put my gun to the supervisor's head.

"Open this shit," Thunder demanded, and I translated it in Spanish.

The Mexican man shook his head, disappointed, with a smirk. He refused to open the trunk.

"Fuck this," Thunder said, then squeezed the trigger—BLOCA! The shot echoed through the house. The supervisor's brains painted the walls. Chunks of brain matter splashed at my feet.

"What the fuck?" I said, mugging Thunder.

All of a sudden, Gold knew the combination to the trunk. It was filled with hundreds. My eyes bucked. We snatched up all the merch and hit the door.

As we exited the house, Thunder spun around. "Wait, we can't leave like this," Thunder said.

He approached Goldy, stuck his gun to his head—*BOCA!*—and head-tapped him.

"Fuck is you doing?" I asked, angrily.

"Leave no witness. I'm securing the bag. These Mexicans are like roaches—they don't die," he said, as he started murdering everyone in the house.

I ran to the car, leaving him to finish. Thunder was a madman, and I wanted no part in his shit. Tires screeched as we got away from the scene. We got back to Waco with all the cash and dope.

I got on Thunder's ass about killing the men inside the house. This shit could come back to haunt us. We sat in the apartment, getting a count on what we'd taken. Thunder and I eased our tension. I still didn't understand his reasoning behind the murders.

Moments later, the count was in. We had 27 kilos of cocaine, 200 thousand in cash, and a Ziploc bag full of little blue pills that none of us knew what they were. Everyone called it a night.

The next day, Flex and I got a start on things. We started by busting down one of the bricks of cocaine. Flex reached out to Remo, a Puerto Rican with the best whip game in the city. Thirty minutes later, he was in the kitchen cooking up one of the kilos. I stood over him and watched. He grabbed the whole key and crushed it down in the blender, then he blended the lidocaine together. I looked and waited while he did his thing. Flex was posted in the other room, playing Xbox. There was only one thing that bothered me: Thunder had murdered the whole house. It would bring some unwanted heat from the cops and the cartel. Thunder was a wild card, and I had to figure out how to deal with him. I would have to go through Flex—that's who had his ear.

Before I knew it, Remo had six ounces of crack laid out on the counter drying. There was more cocaine crammed into the blender, and the pills were still on the counter untouched. I picked them up and examined them.

"What's this?" I asked, curiously wondering why he hadn't touched them yet.

"The blues are fentanyl pills. They're stronger than heroin. We got them in Puerto Rico for twenty dollars a pill. The coke is good—it's definitely ninety percent. You could put the blues on the coke, but I don't see no need. It's already pure. You'll make more if you blend them with some dog, but what's up with this dope? Y'all got more for sale?" he asked.

Flex stepped into the kitchen. "Not for you, nigga. You workin' for us now," he interjected.

"A'ight, I'm with that," he said hesitantly. However, he took the offer. Flex had given him more or less a directive, like he was punking him. "You gon' work for us, shaking this dope," Flex stated.

Tupac and Suge Knight, I thought to myself.

Flex and I left Remo to the kitchen.

"While I got your ear, I need you to talk to Thunder for me," I said, staring at him with a serious glare.

"'Bout what?"

"Last night wasn't cool. Popeye could send a hit squad out here. We can't go to war with no cartel, my nigga."

Flex was understanding at times. He nodded and told me he'd handle it, but couldn't make no promises. That was good enough for me.

Later that day, everyone sat in the small apartment. I explained how I wanted us to expand and take the streets over. It was time. We had formed a conglomerate—minus Kamar, that is. He had to fight the war on so-called terror for President Bush and now, soon-to-be Obama.

"We don't want no outside niggas over here," I said.

It was weird because all of us represented different mobs. Flex and Thunder were both GDs from the Robert Taylors in Chicago, while Kamar and I were Black Disciples. Kamar had put me on; he was from the Calumet Building in Chicago. I was the only one actually from Rockford, originally from Woodlawn and Acorn St. Gambit was a new breed from the Village out of Chicago as well.

"Let's call the projects Waaco," Flex replied.

I looked at him confused. "That's a place in Texas. This is Rockford, fam. Why would you say that?" I asked.

"Because we smoking all our ops. Every nigga outside of us is cowards," Thunder added.

I scrunched my face up. "I'm still not gettin' what that means," I replied, looking for some sort of clarification.

Thunder chuckled. "We assassinate all cowardly organizations. Just like I did the Nunez organization tonight."

I smirked, then said, "All that sounds good coming out your mouth, but you do know they're not gonna take the death of their comrades lightly. They comin' lookin' for this dope," I replied.

Flex rose from his seat. "I'm wit' whatever you niggas wanna do, but right now I gotta meet someone," he said before exiting the room.

"So what's the plan?" Calico asked.

Finally, someone showed some concern. We were playing with fire, and no one took it seriously. I had to answer to all this heat soon. I was the one who dealt with Speedy and Nacho, and they answered to Popeye personally, even though he was in California.

(SPEEDY)

NUNEZ CARTEL . . .

I looked around the house, staring at all the dead bodies inside. One of the men was my cousin, Falco. I walked over to him and cradled his lifeless body. His eyes were open, staring at me. I couldn't believe someone had the balls to rob us. I was one of the most feared men in the city. I was part of the Nunez cartel, ran by the Black Hand, Popeye. I had to report this to my uncle, Nacho. He wasn't going to like hearing that our stash house had been robbed. My henchmen pulled me away from the body.

"Boss, what do you want us to do with all these bodies?" Carlos said.

"Burn them," I replied with no remorse, sharply, then exited the house. I went and sat in my Tahoe. I had to make the dreaded call to Nacho. He would have the honors of talking to Popeye to ask him how he wanted to handle this. He picked up on the first ring.

"Ola," he answered the phone in Spanish.

I began to tell him about the stash, and he became irate. Falco was his son. I knew he wasn't going to like what he'd heard.

"I want them all dead. Set the city on fire and cut the pipeline. There'll be no more drugs until you find out who's responsible," he said.

I listened to every word he spoke carefully. I knew he meant business when it came to his son. It was going to be like finding a needle in a haystack to find the men. Fortunately, we had cameras inside the house, and the dope had trackers on it. I had to go somewhere to use a laptop in order to activate the GPS.

"I'm on it, Uncle. Give me until the end of the day," I replied.

"I don't want the end of the day. I want them now. I got 50 thousand on their heads. I got 250 if you bring them alive. I want them to die slow, day after day," he replied viciously.

I carefully listened to him attentively. I knew I had to comply with his directives as he gave them to me. Nacho wasn't the man to repeat himself. In fact, he hated it. We ended the call. I told my men to burn everyone except for Falco. Popeye would want him to get a proper burial. He would handle the arrangements himself. I pulled away from the stash house.

I needed to get to a laptop in order to bring up the GPS on our dope. I looked at my Rolex—it was getting late. I would get an early start tomorrow.

NEXT DAY . . .

I stroked the keyboard of the laptop. I watched as the GPS screen came up, showing the location of the drugs. My men stood waiting on me to give the order. I jumped out of my seat.

“Load up,” I ordered my men.

We piled into a motorcade of Tahoes and sped off toward the location the drugs had pinged on. I had an AK laid across my lap. Everybody else had Uzis and Mac-90s. I was about to turn the location into Afghanistan. My driver looked over to me and asked, “Are we taking them alive?”

I grinned. “We’ll figure that out when I get there.”

I laid back in the seat and went into deep thought. I hadn’t run a plan that far off in my head. All I saw was blood. When the location pinged, I wanted someone dead for killing my cousin. My uncle was backing me on anything I wanted to do because of his son’s death. This was a tragic time for the city. I was about to paint the city red. As we drove toward the house where I knew one of the bricks was located, I jacked the slide on my AK. As we got closer, the truck was silent. We turned into an apartment complex full of row houses. It was called Black Hawk Projects. The place was livid with drug dealers. We drove down Birch Court. The kids dangerously ran to cars—they were careless. It was hard to believe my GPS located the dope here. I looked at the numbers on all the apartments. I searched for 1502 Birch. We sat behind tinted windows. No one knew who was in the trucks.

“That’s it right there,” I pointed at the apartment with all the young boys out front.

“Hmm,” I thought for a moment.

“We don’t got a minute. These niggas gonna recognize us soon,” Thotcho said.

And he was right. We were getting a lot of stares. Some were already clutching their guns.

"Ride back through, see if I recognize any of them. One of the men took their mask off while in the house," I said. The house was set up with surveillance, and I went over the camera footage this morning while I viewed the GPS. I got on my chirp and let the motorcade know they could pull away. I had a plan. We rode past the house where the GPS had located the dope, then parked around the corner and waited for a fiend to pull up. A guy came strutting up 11th Street as we sat parked at McDonald's. I offered him a hundred dollars to go to the door and lure one of the men to the truck's window.

"You actually think this shit's gonna work?" Thotcho asked with much skepticism.

"You worry too much, my friend. These niggas are greedy. We need to take my uncle a prize," I said.

Thotcho chuckled, then we waited for the dope fiend to return.

(CALICO)

Willy Key came to the door. I looked him up and down. "Fuck yo hype ass want?" I said. I knew his broke ass ain't have shit. Everyone in the house laughed at him. Willy Key used to be part of our crew until he started smoking crack. I got him hooked on the dope after I found out he was fucking one of my bitches. Willy Key and I didn't get along at all. I don't know why he even showed his face here.

"Say bruh, it's some Mexicans outside right now. They got money. These mufukas lookin' to spend," he said.

I let the words sit on me for a second. I'd stolen the kilo from the robbery—Zamad and Flex, no one knew I had it. I planned on making some extra money outside of Waaco. I grabbed my Glock off the refrigerator. I decided to check it out. I might be able to rob them as well. Mexican smokers were known to keep a lot of weed.

I walked up the block. I could barely see the truck from here. He said they'll be… Willy Key walked off in a separate direction. I got closer to the truck, my head on a swivel. A Tahoe drove up fast. The doors flew open, and I upped my pipe.

Boca!

The shot echoed. I must've hit one of them because a body was quickly discarded from the truck. Another SUV blocked me in from the front. They had poles aimed at me. *Bloc! Bloc! Bloc!* They fired shots at me. I was struck once in the leg. I fell to the pavement and blacked out.

When I woke, I was tied to a long beam. I jerked and moved as I came to the realization of what had happened. Three men stood around me like sharks in water. In front of me was the kilo I had taken from the house. I knew shit was about to get ugly for me. I silently wondered if they'd murked Monique, my BM, at the house to get the dope. That was a stupid thought. I shook my head, knowing that bitch ass nigga Willy Key knew something was up. I vowed to kill that mufuka if I got out of this alive.

(ZAMAD)

The projects was booming with traffic. Word had got out that the Mexicans weren't selling no more coke in the city until Thunder was turned over. They now knew who he was. He had a million-dollar bounty on his head. I listened as one of our men gave us the news.

"Man, they shutting our water off," one of my soldiers pouted.

"What you think, fam?" I asked in a calm tone. Thunder could care less. He looked at me, shrugged, and went back to playing his game. He had no remorse. I went back to bagging up the dope we'd took from them. I finished up at the table. *Vrm, vrm, vrm,* my phone buzzed on the table. It was Kamar.

"Oh, fuck. I forgot," I said, realizing I was supposed to take him to the airport. The young kid looked at me confused. I knew he probably thought we needed the Mexicans' dope, but we were sitting good.

"Check it out," I said and walked him to the back. I showed him all the dope we'd took and looked him in the eye. "They need us, we don't need them," I said, narrowing my eyes.

Vrm, vrm, vrm — my phone buzzed again. It was Kamar.

"Oh shit," I uttered, forgetting I was supposed to take him to the airport.

"What's good, fam?" I answered, knowing he was gonna be upset.

"Zamad, where yawl at?" he said frantically.

"Was up, you aight?" I asked, perking up to attention. Kamar and I were like brothers. I wouldn't dare let anything happen to him, and vice versa for me.

"Nah, bruh. They got Calico."

"What! Who?" I said in a concerned tone.

"The cartel, and they know who Thunder is," he replied, but we already knew that.

"Fuck how—matter of fact, squash that shit. Where you at?"

"At home. They got that shit buzzing on MySpace."

I racked my brain, thinking of how they got onto Thunder. Had it been Calico, there'd have been a thousand gualos outside Waaco trying to get in right now. Vrm, vrm, vrm — my phone buzzed as we stood in the middle of Rene's living room. I looked at the ID tag. It was unknown. Thunder glanced at me.

"Who is it?" he asked as the phone buzzed. I could feel what was to come through my phone.

I shrugged with a ghastly stare. Vrm, vrm, vrm.

"Answer it," Thunder said, bringing me back to reality.

"Hello."

“Ola, poppy. You have something that belongs to me,” a man said in a strong Spanish dialect.

I stared into space, thinking of something to say. Then Thunder snatched the phone.

“We ready for whatever. Y’all got my homie, and we want him back,” he spat into the phone, not caring to know whom he was even speaking to.

Thunder hit the speaker button, and I recognized the voice as Speedy. He didn’t know who he was calling; otherwise, he would’ve said my name, so I let Thunder continue to talk to him. They went back and forth for a minute. Speedy demanded their dope back in exchange for Calico.

“What now?” he asked. Everyone looked to me for answers.

“One thing for sure, they gonna kill him, so it ain’t no reason to give the dope up. Let me think for a second.” I was the brains of our operations. I believed strongly in the 5 P’s: Proper Preparation Prevents Poor Performance, which is what baffled me about this situation. I couldn’t think how they got onto us this quick. We were all masked up except for Thunder, who slid his off during the lick. Then it dawned on me — they must’ve had cameras inside the house. That’s how they knew who he was and not any of us. Kamar was scheduled to fly out to Afghanistan today. I rose from my seat to take him to O’Hare. After that, I would handle this shit with them when I got back to Rockford. Kamar didn’t need to stay with us—they would try to court-martial him if he didn’t show up.

“I’m gonna talk to O’Riley and see about some guns. I’m sure he’ll extend a hand for me,” I said.

“You think them racist mufukas gonna do anything to help a nigga? You better think twice about that, my G,” Thunder shot back.

Thunder didn’t know the relationship I had with them, and I surely wasn’t about to expose my hand to him.

“Just let me handle it. I’m sure they’ll listen to what I got to say,” I said, then rose from my seat to leave. I stepped outside. The frigid air gave me a dose of reality. I slid into my Magnum and hurriedly hit the heater, rubbing my hands together. The music boomed as the car came to life. Jeezy blared through the fifteen-inch L7s in my trunk. I made the trip alone to O’Hare, then I would see the Irish afterwards.

3 HOURS LATER...

After I dropped Kamar off, I pulled up to the Lucky 7 bar. I walked in through the side door where they held all the gambling. When I entered, I was met at the door by a massive wall of a redhead white man.

“Z, how's it going? What brings you down?” he said in a friendly gesture, then offered up his hand for a shake.

“Is O'Riley in?” I asked. He led the way to where O'Riley was parked. I slid into the booth across from him.

“I got a small problem, maybe you can help me with.”

O'Riley leaned back in his seat and grinned. He clasped his hands together. “What can I do for you?”

“I'm having some beef with the Nunez cartel. Popeye's son got hit, and he thinks my people had something to do with it,” I said, explaining everything to him—of course, leaving out some details. O'Riley's face twitched. I knew he was fuming. He hated Popeye. They’d had this feud going on for some years. It was O'Riley who put me onto the Nunez cartel. I'd never met Popeye personally—Speedy was my connection—but Popeye lived in California. We'd never met, which was good. The Irish mob hated the cartel. I knew it wouldn’t be a problem for them to help me with this situation.

“I can help you with this, but it’s going to cost you,” O'Riley replied.

“It always does. How much? Or should I say, what do you want?”

“We want some of that business you got on the west side.”

I stared off, as if to say I couldn't make it happen. O'Riley must've read my body language.

"Problem?" he shot back.

"Thing is, I can't make that determination for you to move in like that. Everyone knows you guys detest blacks, so it could be a very uncomfortable situation."

"Ha! Ha! That's an understatement coming from you. Business is business. We deal with you, you're black, aren't you?"

I took the hint of sarcasm in his tone. "Don't put me in that position to make this determination," I replied, skeptical of the outcome.

He perked upward and rested on his arms. Just as he was about to speak, O'Mally walked up, carving an apple. He was the real one in charge of the Irish mob, from Rockford to Chicago.

"What's the problem you come to us with?" he said in a calming but menacing voice.

I looked to O'Riley. He nodded, and I went to explain.

"The cartel snatched my friend up, and I need your help to get him back. You guys got the guns to go up against them. I don't," I said sharply.

"O'Riley, what do you think?" O'Mally asked, biting into his fruit calmly.

"I think we need a bigger slice of the pie, but our friend here seems to think it may be too much," he replied.

"Not too much, just harder to obtain on my own. There's a lot more players to deal with, other than me. That could cause a war between us."

"Hmm. I'm sure you'll work things out," O'Mally said, then walked away.

I got a venomous vibe about O'Mally. He was like a demonic angel, preying on the weak, using people's fear as a control mechanism. They were playing hardball. I knew this wouldn't come cheap, but offering him real estate in our neighborhoods was out of the question. However, it was negotiable.

"I can give you guys a ten percent kickback," I said.

"Make it fifteen, and I'll guarantee you the cops won't bother you," he said.

I gave him an awkward look. "How can you make me that promise?"

"I got a cop that's on my payroll. I can make this thing with the Nunez cartel go away as quick as it came to you. Judging by what you said, your boy may have signed his death wish."

I agreed to his fifteen percent deal and exited in a hurry. As I drove home to retrieve the payment for the Irish, I thought about the deal.

I got home and went straight to the basement. My wife must've followed me down. I felt a presence behind me and spun around. She was always concerned about what happened to me in the streets. I'd met her through O'Riley. We had one child together; he was eight years old. She was mixed with Irish, Italian, and Black. My son's skin was caramel-colored. I was happy about that. She startled me as I spun to face her.

"Baby, we need to talk," she said with concern in her voice.

"I got some business to tend to right now. It's got to wait," I replied, as I counted out the money from my safe. She looked down at what I had on the floor.

"What's all that for?" she asked.

"I got some shit to handle with the Irish."

"No, that's what it's about. You gotta leave them alone," she said.

"We'll talk when I get back," I said, then put their payment in a book bag. I kissed her on the cheek and bolted up the steps, leaving her standing there.

As I drove back to the pub, I had it made up in my mind. Thunder had started this whole shit with his antics. I knew how to solve my problem. I was about to collect that ticket he had on him. For a man, a nigga would do his own mama.

(TAESHA)

I walked back upstairs from the basement. Zamad had come in so quick, I didn't know how to tell him what I knew. I vowed to tell him once I had a chance. I just hoped it wasn't too late. He'd left in a hurry, and I hadn't had a chance to fill him in on what was really going on. He and I had grown attached to each other.

Vrm, vrm, vrm—my phone buzzed on the table. I looked at the screen; it was Kamar. I huffed before I answered.

"What's up?" I answered.

"I'm at the airport. Did you talk to Zamad yet?" he asked.

I scoffed before I replied. "No, I can't right now. He's about to meet up with the Irish."

"Okay, then can you hold off until I get back? I don't want to put too much on him right now. There's a lot going on, and it may be too much for one man to bear," he said.

I honestly didn't know if he could handle any of what was being put on him. I agreed with Kamar, then flipped my phone closed. I sat on the couch in deep thought. I had the weight of the world on my shoulders. I had some things to tell Zamad. I knew he wouldn't handle them well. How could I tell my son's father that I had an affair with his friend? And not to mention, he is under a federal indictment with the feds. I didn't think things would go this far, but now they were asking me to come forward. O'Riley worked with the feds, and he helped put me in with Zamad. Now, 8 and a half years later, the favor was being called in. Our relationship was all a lie. I'd grown on Zamad, and I couldn't turn on him. But I had to warn him of the danger, even if it put me in danger. I didn't know how he'd take it.

(ZARO)

PRESENT DAY . . .

I sat in the courtroom on fire. Frank hadn't showed up, and I let this public pretender talk me into taking the fool's mate plea agreement. However, I wouldn't be in jail for long. The judge told me to stand. The state's attorney sat on the opposite side of the room, looking like the nerd. He smirked at me, knowing he had won. Curly Abbotts and his partner were in the jury box. It was a small win for them. They didn't care how they'd got it.

"Mr. Smith, you are charged with the murder of Tiffany Harris. Do you understand these charges?" the judge asked, looking at me over the top of his wire-frame glasses.

"Yes, I do, Your Honor," I replied politely. I felt like a lame. My lawyer was MIA, and I'd put that work in for him basically for free. It was cool, because now he was on my list.

"I understand you signed into a binding plea agreement. You do understand I'm going to sentence you today. Your range of sentence will vary between thirty years to life. This is a Class X felony."

Suddenly, the time I signed to had grown outside of what I was tricked into pleading guilty to, and now I was being railroaded because my attorney wasn't present.

"I don't understand. I thought I was looking at five years."

"I'm sorry, Mr. Smith, this is a murder case, and this deal wasn't conveyed to me. You are bound to these terms of the agreement."

My public defender whispered in my ear. "If you buck now, the state will use your plea against you and double the number. Besides, the detectives just produced a door cam that caught you leaving the scene in a Magnum and some audio from a credible informant. It's up to you. If you go to trial, it will be bad for you," she said, then stared at me like she was on their side.

That door cam was enough. If they knew I was in the Magnum, it was solid, compelling evidence on me. But the informant and audio were something to think about. I knew

I was cooked, but that bitch had me fucked up. I wanted to smack fire from that nasty, pretty-ass bitch.

I stared at that fine-ass bitch with disgust. Suddenly, she began to look like a troll. I shook my head, defeated.

"What the fuck? You knew this already. You tricked me into signing that shit," I said, making a spectacle in court. I looked over to the prosecutor, and he had a smug grin on his face, like they had robbed me of my freedom. The judge began to speak, and I blocked out everything he said. All I heard was him saying he was ready to pass my sentence down.

Suddenly, the doors to the courtroom burst open. Frank walked in, wheeling a folder.

"I have new, compelling evidence to exonerate my client. May I approach, Your Honor?" he asked, already heading that way.

I looked at Frank as he walked past me. He winked at me, then smiled. The courtroom erupted into chatter. I hoped it wasn't too late. I couldn't take the plea back. Not to mention, the evidence they had on me was enough to get me convicted. The state's attorney sat looking at me with a smirk. He knew there was no way out for me.

To be continued

Lock Down Publications and Ca$h Presents Assisted Publishing Packages

Due to an increase in the price of services we have increased our prices. The prices below reflect the price increase as of 11/1/24.

BASIC PACKAGE **$699** Editing Cover Design Formatting	**UPGRADED PACKAGE** **$1000** Typing Editing Cover Design Formatting Upload eBooks to Amazon Upload Paperback to Amazon
ADVANCE PACKAGE **$1,400** Typing Editing (line editing/content) Cover Design Formatting Copyright Registration Proofreading Upload eBooks to Amazon Upload Paperback to Amazon	**LDP SUPREME PACKAGE** **$1,700** Typing Editing (line editing/content) Cover Design Formatting Copyright Registration Proofreading Set up Amazon Account Upload eBooks to Amazon Upload Paperback to Amazon Advertise on LDP's Amazon and Facebook Page

***

Other services available upon request.
Additional charges may apply

Submission Guideline

Submit the first three chapters of your completed manuscript to ldpsubmissions@gmail.com. In the subject line add **Your Book's Title**. The manuscript must be in a Word Doc file and sent as an attachment. Document should be in Times New Roman, double spaced, and in size 12 font. Also, provide your synopsis and full contact information. If sending multiple submissions, they must each be in a separate email.

Have a story but no way to send it electronically? You can still submit to LDP/Ca$h Presents. Send in the first three chapters, written or typed, of your completed manuscript to:

LDP: Submissions Dept
P.O. Box 944
Stockbridge, GA 30281-9998

DO NOT send original manuscript. Must be a duplicate. Provide your synopsis and a cover letter containing your full contact information.

Thanks for considering LDP and Ca$h Presents.

NEW RELEASES

BLOODLINE OF A SAVAGE 1-3
THESE VICIOUS STREETS 1-3
RELENTLESS GOON 1-3
BY PRINCE A. TAUHID

THE BUTTERFLY MAFIA 1-3
BY FUMIYA PAYNE

A THUG'S STREET PRINCESS 1&2
BY MEESHA

CITY OF SMOKE 3
BY MOLOTTI

GET IT IN SLUGS 1 &2
BY B. STALL

STANDING ON HER BUSINESS 1&2
BY DG SANTANA

STEPPERS 1,2&3
THE REAL BADDIES OF CHI-RAQ
BY KING RIO

THE LANE 1&2
BY KEN-KEN SPENCE

THUG OF SPADES 1&2
LOVE IN THE TRENCHES 2
CORNER BOYS
BY COREY ROBINSON

TIL DEATH 3
BY ARYANNA

DRILL CITY | ZAY'TOWVEN

THE BIRTH OF A GANGSTER 4
BY DELMONT PLAYER

PRODUCT OF THE STREETS 1-3
BY DEMOND "MONEY" ANDERSON

NO TIME FOR ERROR
BY KEESE

MONEY HUNGRY DEMONS 1-2
BY TRANAY ADAMS

HUB CITY MENACE 1-3
BY J. WHITE

A THUGGISH PASSION 1&2
LAND OF DA HOOLIGANZ 1-4
KILLAZ ON STANDBY 1&2
BY IRA B.

FO'EVA ROLLIN 1&2
BY ASSA RAYMOND BAKER

THE LEVEL UP 1&3
BY LUXURY KING

Coming Soon from Lock Down Publications/Ca$h Presents

IF YOU CROSS ME ONCE 6
ANGEL V
By Anthony Fields

A THUGS STREET PRINCESS 3
By Meesha

CORNER BOYS 2
By Corey Robinson

THA TAKEOVER
By Keith Chandler

BETRAYAL OF A G 2
By Ray Vinci

SAVAGE FAMILY EMPIRE 1&2
SOULLESS GOON 1,2&3
THE DIRTY SIDE OF MONEY 1,2&3
By Prince

FOR MY ENEMY'S SAKE
AMBITIONS OF A SLIDER
FRESH OFF DA PORCH
By IRA B.

BY THE TRUCKLOAD 1-4
TIPPIN' THE SCALES 1-3
BAD BITCHES WIT GUNZ 3
PROBLEM SOLVED 2
By Christopher "Diesel" Hornezes

Available Now

RESTRAINING ORDER 1 & 2
By **CA$H & Coffee**

LOVE KNOWS NO BOUNDARIES 1-3
By **Coffee**

RAISED AS A GOON I, II, III & IV
BRED BY THE SLUMS I, II, III
BLAST FOR ME I & II
ROTTEN TO THE CORE I II III
A BRONX TALE I, II, III
DUFFLE BAG CARTEL I II III IV V VI
HEARTLESS GOON I II III IV V
A SAVAGE DOPEBOY I II
DRUG LORDS I II III
CUTTHROAT MAFIA I II
KING OF THE TRENCHES
By **Ghost**

LAY IT DOWN I & II
LAST OF A DYING BREED I II
BLOOD STAINS OF A SHOTTA I & II III
By **Jamaica**

LOYAL TO THE GAME I II III
LIFE OF SIN I, II III
By **TJ & Jelissa**

IF LOVING HIM IS WRONG…I & II
LOVE ME EVEN WHEN IT HURTS I II III
By **Jelissa**

PUSH IT TO THE LIMIT
By **Bre' Hayes**

DRILL CITY | ZAY'TOWVEN

BLOODY COMMAS I & II
SKI MASK CARTEL I, II & III
KING OF NEW YORK I II, III IV V
RISE TO POWER I II III
COKE KINGS I II III IV V
BORN HEARTLESS I II III IV
KING OF THE TRAP I II
By **T.J. Edwards**

WHEN THE STREETS CLAP BACK I & II III
THE HEART OF A SAVAGE I II III IV
MONEY MAFIA I II
LOYAL TO THE SOIL I II III
By **Jibril Williams**

A DISTINGUISHED THUG STOLE MY HEART I II & III
LOVE SHOULDN'T HURT I II III IV
RENEGADE BOYS 1-4
PAID IN KARMA 1-3
SAVAGE STORMS 1-3
AN UNFORESEEN LOVE 1-3
BABY, I'M WINTERTIME COLD 1-3
A THUG'S STREET PRINCESS 1&2
By **Meesha**

A GANGSTER'S CODE 1-3
A GANGSTER'S SYN 1-3
THE SAVAGE LIFE 1-3
CHAINED TO THE STREETS 1-3
BLOOD ON THE MONEY 1-3
A GANGSTA'S PAIN 1-3
BEAUTIFUL LIES AND UGLY TRUTHS
CHURCH IN THESE STREETS
By **J-Blunt**

CUM FOR ME 1-8
An LDP Erotica Collaboration

DRILL CITY | ZAY'TOWVEN

BLOOD OF A BOSS 1-5
SHADOWS OF THE GAME
TRAP BASTARD
By **Askari**

THE STREETS BLEED MURDER 1-3
THE HEART OF A GANGSTA 1-3
By **Jerry Jackson**

WHEN A GOOD GIRL GOES BAD
By **Adrienne**

THE COST OF LOYALTY 1-3
By **Kweli**

BRIDE OF A HUSTLA 1-3
THE FETTI GIRLS 1-3
CORRUPTED BY A GANGSTA 1-4
BLINDED BY HIS LOVE
THE PRICE YOU PAY FOR LOVE 1-3
DOPE GIRL MAGIC 1-3
By **Destiny Skai**

A KINGPIN'S AMBITION
A KINGPIN'S AMBITION II
I MURDER FOR THE DOUGH
By **Ambitious**

TRUE SAVAGE 1-7
DOPE BOY MAGIC 1-3
MIDNIGHT CARTEL 1-3
CITY OF KINGZ 1&2
NIGHTMARE ON SILENT AVE
THE PLUG OF LIL MEXICO 1&2
CLASSIC CITY
By **Chris Green**

DRILL CITY | ZAY'TOWVEN

A GANGSTER'S REVENGE 1-4
THE BOSS MAN'S DAUGHTERS 1-5
A SAVAGE LOVE 1&2
BAE BELONGS TO ME 1&2
A HUSTLER'S DECEIT 1-3
WHAT BAD BITCHES DO 1-3
SOUL OF A MONSTER 1-3
KILL ZONE
A DOPE BOY'S QUEEN 1-3
TIL DEATH 1-3
IMMA DIE BOUT MINE 1-6
DYING FOR LIKES
By **Aryanna**

A DOPEBOY'S PRAYER
By **Eddie "Wolf" Lee**

THE KING CARTEL 1-3
By **Frank Gresham**

THESE NIGGAS AIN'T LOYAL 1-3
By **Nikki Tee**

GANGSTA SHYT 1-3
By **CATO**

THE ULTIMATE BETRAYAL
By **Phoenix**

BOSS'N UP 1-3
By **Royal Nicole**

I LOVE YOU TO DEATH
By **Destiny J**

I RIDE FOR MY HITTA
I STILL RIDE FOR MY HITTA
By **Misty Holt**

DRILL CITY | ZAY'TOWVEN

LOVE & CHASIN' PAPER
By **Qay Crockett**

TO DIE IN VAIN
SINS OF A HUSTLA
By **ASAD**

BROOKLYN HUSTLAZ
By **Boogsy Morina**

BROOKLYN ON LOCK 1 & 2
By **Sonovia**

GANGSTA CITY
By **Teddy Duke**

A DRUG KING AND HIS DIAMOND 1-3
A DOPEMAN'S RICHES
HER MAN, MINE'S TOO 1&2
CASH MONEY HO'S
THE WIFEY I USED TO BE 1&2
PRETTY GIRLS DO NASTY THINGS
By **Nicole Goosby**

LIPSTICK KILLAH 1-3
CRIME OF PASSION 1-3
FRIEND OR FOE 1-3
By **Mimi**

TRAPHOUSE KING 1-3
KINGPIN KILLAZ 1-3
STREET KINGS 1&2
PAID IN BLOOD 1&2
CARTEL KILLAZ 1-3
DOPE GODS 1&2
By **Hood Rich**

THE STREETS ARE CALLING
By **Duquie Wilson**

STEADY MOBBN' 1-3
THE STREETS STAINED MY SOUL 1-3
By **Marcellus Allen**

WHO SHOT YA 1-3
SON OF A DOPE FIEND 1-4
HEAVEN GOT A GHETTO 1&2
SKI MASK MONEY 1&2
By **Renta**

GORILLAZ IN THE BAY 1-4
TEARS OF A GANGSTA 1/&2
3X KRAZY 1&2
STRAIGHT BEAST MODE 1&2
By **DE'KARI**

TRIGGADALE 1-3
MURDA WAS THE CASE 1-3
By **Elijah R. Freeman**

SLAUGHTER GANG 1-3
RUTHLESS HEART 1-3
By **Willie Slaughter**

GOD BLESS THE TRAPPERS 1-3
THESE SCANDALOUS STREETS 1-3
FEAR MY GANGSTA 1-5
THESE STREETS DON'T LOVE NOBODY 1-2
BURY ME A G 1-5
A GANGSTA'S EMPIRE 1-4
THE DOPEMAN'S BODYGAURD 1&2
THE REALEST KILLAZ 1-3
THE LAST OF THE OGS 1-3
By **Tranay Adams**

MARRIED TO A BOSS 1-3
By **Destiny Skai & Chris Green**

KINGZ OF THE GAME 1-7
CRIME BOSS 1-4
By **Playa Ray**

FUK SHYT
By **Blakk Diamond**

DON'T F#CK WITH MY HEART 1&2
By **Linnea**

ADDICTED TO THE DRAMA 1-3
IN THE ARM OF HIS BOSS
By **Jamila**

LOYALTY AIN'T PROMISED 1&2
By **Keith Williams**

YAYO 1-4
A SHOOTER'S AMBITION 1&2
BRED IN THE GAME
By **S. Allen**

TRAP GOD 1-3
RICH $AVAGE 1-3
MONEY IN THE GRAVE 1-3
CARTEL MONEY 1&2
By **Martell Troublesome Bolden**

FOREVER GANGSTA 1&2
GLOCKS ON SATIN SHEETS 1&2
By **Adrian Dulan**

TOE TAGZ 1-4
LEVELS TO THIS SHYT 1&2
IT'S JUST ME AND YOU
By **Ah'Million**

DRILL CITY | ZAY'TOWVEN

KINGPIN DREAMS 1-3
RAN OFF ON DA PLUG
By **Paper Boi Rari**

THE STREETS MADE ME 1-3
By **Larry D. Wright**

CONFESSIONS OF A GANGSTA 1-4
CONFESSIONS OF A JACKBOY 1-3
CONFESSIONS OF A HITMAN
CONFESSIONS OF A DOPE BOY
By **Nicholas Lock**

I'M NOTHING WITHOUT HIS LOVE
SINS OF A THUG
TO THE THUG I LOVED BEFORE
A GANGSTA SAVED XMAS
IN A HUSTLER I TRUST
By **Monet Dragun**

QUIET MONEY 1-3
THUG LIFE 1-3
EXTENDED CLIP 1&2
A GANGSTA'S PARADISE
By **Trai'Quan**

CAUGHT UP IN THE LIFE 1-3
THE STREETS NEVER LET GO 1-3
By **Robert Baptiste**

NEW TO THE GAME 1-3
MONEY, MURDER & MEMORIES 1-3
By **Malik D. Rice**

CREAM 2-3
THE STREETS WILL TALK
By **Yolanda Moore**

THE STREETS WILL NEVER CLOSE 1-3
By **K'ajji**

LIFE OF A SAVAGE 1-4
A GANGSTA'S QUR'AN 1-4
MURDA SEASON 1-3
GANGLAND CARTEL 1-3
CHI'RAQ GANGSTAS 1-4
KILLERS ON ELM STREET 1-3
JACK BOYZ N DA BRONX 1-3
A DOPEBOY'S DREAM 1-3
JACK BOYS VS DOPE BOYS 1-3
COKE GIRLZ
COKE BOYS
SOSA GANG 1&2
BRONX SAVAGES
BODYMORE KINGPINS
BLOOD OF A GOON
By **Romell Tukes**

CONCRETE KILLA 1-3
VICIOUS LOYALTY 1-3
BLOODY MONEY BAGS
By **Kingpen**

THE ULTIMATE SACRIFICE 1-6
KHADIFI
IF YOU CROSS ME ONCE 1-3
ANGEL 1-4
IN THE BLINK OF AN EYE
By **Anthony Fields**

THE LIFE OF A HOOD STAR
By **Ca$h & Rashia Wilson**

NIGHTMARES OF A HUSTLA 1-3
BLOOD AND GAMES 1&2
By **King Dream**

GHOST MOB
By **Stilloan Robinson**

HARD AND RUTHLESS 1&2
MOB TOWN 251
THE BILLIONAIRE BENTLEYS 1-3
REAL G'S MOVE IN SILENCE
By **Von Diesel**

MOB TIES 1-7
SOUL OF A HUSTLER, HEART OF A KILLER 1-3
GORILLAZ IN THE TRENCHES
OOPS CRY TOO 1&2
THE DAUGHTER OF A CARTEL BOSS
By **SayNoMore**

BODYMORE MURDERLAND 1-3
THE BIRTH OF A GANGSTER 1-4
By **Delmont Player**

FOR THE LOVE OF A BOSS 1&2
By **C. D. Blue**

KILLA KOUNTY 1-5
TENDER
By **Khufu**

MOBBED UP 1-4
THE BRICK MAN 1-5
THE COCAINE PRINCESS 1-10
STEPPERS 1-3
SUPER GREMLIN 1-4
A GANGSTA'S SON
By **King Rio**

MONEY GAME 1&2
By **Smoove Dolla**

DRILL CITY | ZAY'TOWVEN

A GANGSTA'S KARMA 1-5
By **FLAME**

KING OF THE TRENCHES 1-3
By **GHOST & TRANAY ADAMS**

BAD BITCHES WIT GUNZ 1&2
PROBLEM SOLVED
By "Christopher Diesel" Hornezes

QUEEN OF THE ZOO 1&2
By **Black Migo**

GRIMEY WAYS 1-3
BETRAYAL OF A G
By **Ray Vinci**

XMAS WITH AN ATL SHOOTER
By **Ca$h & Destiny Skai**

KING KILLA 1&2
By **Vincent "Vitto" Holloway**

BETRAYAL OF A THUG 1&2
By **Fre$h**

COUNTDOWN OF A KILLA 1&2
SEX, MURDER AND GOD 1&2
GUNS DOWN, BOTTOMS UP 1&2
By Lo-Life

THE MURDER QUEENS 1-7
By **Michael Gallon**

FOR THE LOVE OF BLOOD 1-4
By **Jamel Mitchell**

DRILL CITY | ZAY'TOWVEN

HOOD CONSIGLIERE 1&2
NO TIME FOR ERROR
By **Keese**

PROTÉGÉ OF A LEGEND 1,2&3
LOVE IN THE TRENCHES 1&2
By **Corey Robinson**

THE PLUG'S RUTHLESS DAUGHTER 1&2
By **Tony Daniels**

BORN IN THE GRAVE 1-3
CRIME PAYS
By **Self Made Tay**

MOAN IN MY MOUTH
By **XTASY**

TORN BETWEEN A GANGSTER AND A GENTLEMAN
By **J-BLUNT & Miss Kim**

LOYALTY IS EVERYTHING 1-3
CITY OF SMOKE 1-3
By **Molotti**

HERE TODAY GONE TOMORROW 1&2
By **Fly Rock**

WOMEN LIE MEN LIE 1-4
FIFTY SHADES OF SNOW 1-3
STACK BEFORE YOU SPLURGE
GIRLS FALL LIKE DOMINOES
NAÏVE TO THE STREETS
By **ROY MILLIGAN**

PILLOW PRINCESS
By **S. Hawkins**

DRILL CITY | ZAY'TOWVEN

THE BUTTERFLY MAFIA 1-3
SALUTE MY SAVAGERY 1&2
By **Fumiya Payne**

THE LANE 1&2
By Ken-Ken Spence

THE PUSSY TRAP 1-5
By **Nene Capri**

DIRTY DNA
By **Blaque**

SANCTIFIED AND HORNY
by **XTASY**

BOOKS BY LDP'S CEO, CA$H

TRUST IN NO MAN
TRUST IN NO MAN 2
TRUST IN NO MAN 3
BONDED BY BLOOD
SHORTY GOT A THUG
THUGS CRY
THUGS CRY 2
THUGS CRY 3
TRUST NO BITCH
TRUST NO BITCH 2
TRUST NO BITCH 3
TIL MY CASKET DROPS
RESTRAINING ORDER
RESTRAINING ORDER 2
IN LOVE WITH A CONVICT
LIFE OF A HOOD STAR
XMAS WITH AN ATL SHOOTER

www.ingramcontent.com/pod-product-compliance
Lightning Source LLC
LaVergne TN
LVHW010913110826
845149LV00013B/2340

* 9 7 8 1 9 7 1 7 7 0 0 9 3 *